D1254101

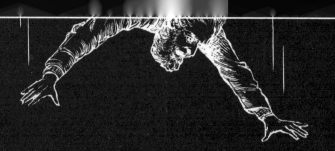

INHERITED DISORDERS

....

INHERITED

{ *Stories, Parables & Problems* }

DISORDERS

ADAM EHRLICH SACHS

Regan Arts.

NEW YORK

Many thanks to Amelia Atlas at ICM and Lucas Wittmann at Regan Arts

Regan Arts.

65 Bleecker Street
New York, NY 10012

First Regan Arts hardcover edition, May 2016.

Library of Congress Control Number: 2015958511

ISBN 978-1-68245-015-4

Jacket design by Richard Ljoenes

Printed in the United States of America

10 9 8 7 6 5 4 3 2 1

{ FOR MY FATHER }

. . . .

INHERITED DISORDERS

....

THE NATURE POET

· ·

A postwar Austrian poet—whose name you might not recognize but who was in his time a fairly prominent figure on the Viennese scene, a fixture of the literary circle at Café Raimund—struggled most of his career to free his poetry from the shadow of his father, a Nazi officer. No one suspected the son of any Nazi sympathies; he even married a Jewish woman. The problem, rather, was that all of his poetry was interpreted by critics as a meditation on his father's crimes. In truth, he had no interest in his father, really no interest in the past at all. He cared about nature: mountains, creeks, ferns. He called himself, at various points, a *creekpoet* or *fernpoet*. Yet every creek, every fern, was construed by his critics—from his very first major review in *Die Zeit* in 1968—as a "reckoning" with the actions of his father, who had once shot 150 Hungarian Jews in one day with his own pistol. The critic noted the total absence in the poet's poems of people, history, politics, fathers, et cetera, and saw their absence as a sign that they were actually the poet's primary concerns, the unspeakable void at the center of his ferns. (The review was *extremely* positive.)

Of course the poet deplored his father's actions. But his "primary concerns" were mountains, creeks, and, especially, ferns.

Over the next decade he published two more acclaimed volumes of nature poetry. Both were interpreted as oblique meditations on his father's crimes.

His fourth volume of nature poetry came out in 1985. It, too, was interpreted as an oblique meditation on his father's crimes, but the reviews were less rapturous than before. The critic for the *Süddeutsche Zeitung* wondered if the poet had anything *else* to write about, anything *besides* his father's wartime crimes, now more than forty years old. "The highly circumscribed nature of his interests," wrote the critic, "became apparent with his second volume and glaring with his third. Now, with his *fourth* consecutive collection of poems to ponder how one generation's crimes burden the next, it has finally become a liability."

For the next thirty years the poet published nothing at all.

His friends began to suspect he was dead, presumably by his own hand. Everyone else forgot about him altogether.

But we now know that he never stopped writing. In fact, he had embarked upon his most ambitious project.

Since every description of a fern had been interpreted as an oblique meditation on his father's crimes, he would write an epic poem about his father's brutal crimes that was actually, obliquely, a description of a single fern. He knew the fern he wanted to describe. It grew on the fringes of a clearing in the woods near his home. A lovely fern. To describe it was easy. By now, that was nothing. But to describe it without mentioning the woods, the clearing, or the fern, to use only words that told how his father executed 150 Hungarian Jews, and yet to implant in his reader's mind, by the time he finished reading the poem, an accurate and even quite detailed image of this one particular fern near his home: *that* was hard. He wanted his reader to close the book, this exhausting, appalling, tragic, merciless book, and have nothing in his head—no ideas, no horrors, no faces, no place names, no characters, no concepts, no morals—nothing but the precise image of a specific fern. He wanted the reader to think to himself: "I just read about the Holocaust. Why am I picturing this fern? What is the *matter* with me?" Such was the literary effect he was aiming for.

When he told his wife his idea, she left him.

The composition of the poem occupied the last thirty years of the poet's life. In the first decade he contemplated his dead father, reading his journals and researching his savage Hungarian campaign, with special attention to the atrocities of June 1, 1941. The subsequent decade was devoted to careful contemplation of the fern: sketching the plant, scribbling notes, often simply sitting there staring at it. In the final decade of his life, the nature poet tried to describe the fern through a narrative poem about his father's June 1st depravity.

This year he finally published *The Kistelek Massacre*. He died the night before its publication, uncertain whether he had succeeded in his aim. He would have treasured this morning's brief review in *Die Zeit*, which simply calls *The Kistelek Massacre* "an elegant evocation of a fern."

{ 2 }

ABOVE AND BEYOND

....

The University of Chicago, where his father had been first a professor and then president, wrote to ask him whether he would consider posing for a sculptor who would be erecting a statue of his father in the classics quadrangle. They sent a sketch of the proposed statue: his father striding forward with his left leg, his right hand gripping a volume of Ovid's *Metamorphoses*. The son wrote back that he would not only consider posing for the artist, he would consider standing, himself, in the classics quadrangle in just that position—left leg striding forward, right hand gripping Ovid—for the rest of his life, and would actually even consider rotating continually but imperceptibly so that he was always facing the sun. To this offer, which the son noted went "above and beyond" what they had requested, the University of Chicago did not respond.

THE CHIMNEY SWEEP

. . . .

When, in 1919, Henry Hobson Fowler, the only son of a London chimney sweep, was named Wykeham Professor of Logic at Oxford University, his colleagues marveled openly at his improbable escape from the chimneys of his fathers into the rarefied air of logic and language. And for a time in his early career it really *did* seem that Fowler had torn himself root and branch out of his own past, from that long line of chimney sweeps into which he had been born, even extirpating all traces of his working-class accent.

But either he was still held in the grip of a tenacious ancestral worldview, or the condescending awe of his colleagues awakened in him certain latent ancestral loyalties, or perhaps he simply came to see some symbolic value in his ancestral vocation, for he began around 1922 or 1923 to speak of his approach to philosophy as "a kind of logico-linguistic chimney sweeping," and over time construed this metaphor in an increasingly literal fashion.

For a while it remained purely figurative. "Our task," he told students on the first day of his fall 1923 seminar, according to notes taken by one of them, "is to shimmy up the flue of logic and language and clear it out." In fall 1924, he specified: "We clear out the philosophical flue with, in one hand, our *brush* and, in the other hand, our *scraper*." Fall 1925: "With our brush we sweep away the loose soot, and with our scraper we chip away at the solid soot." According to the seminar notes, a student asked whether Fowler was referring to "a real chimney or a logico-linguistic chimney," and Fowler replied: "A logico-linguistic chimney. The philosophical flue." In a lecture that spring term, Fowler warned: "It is extremely easy to get trapped in the flue and to suffocate from the soot. As you're climbing, you must never jam your knees against your chest, in this position." He showed them. "You'll suffocate, and we may very well have to dismantle the chimney to retrieve your body." Again a student asked, according to the lecture notes, whether he was referring to "an actual chimney or some kind of philosophical chimney," and Fowler replied: "A philosophical chimney."

Starting in the fall term of 1928, Fowler distributed to his seminar students a brush and a scraper and asked them to raise, whenever they were arguing a philosophical point, either the brush, if they were dislodging *loose* logico-linguistic soot, or the scraper, if they were chipping away at *solid* logico-linguistic soot. He himself brought to seminar every week a long, adjustable, articulated rod with a brush head affixed to one end. With your brushes and scrapers and this long, flexible rod, Fowler exhorted them, we shall clear out the philosophical flue.

"Having done so," said Fowler, in one student's notes, "we

mustn't expect the flue to remain clear ever after. Soon, *with use*, it will fill up with ash and soot once again and we shall have to climb up it once more with our brushes and scrapers, our adjustable rods. Such is the nature of chimneys." He fielded from a student the usual question—*are you talking about regular chimneys or logico-linguistic chimneys?*—but replied this time that he did not understand the distinction the student was trying to draw.

"A chimney," said Fowler, "is a chimney. We clear out the soot." He gestured up and down with the long rod. "We clear out the soot."

In late autumn of 1930, a number of Fowler's students complained to the head of the department that most of their seminars were now spent clearing out chimneys around Oxford, work which was dirty, dangerous, and not conspicuously philosophical in nature. Yesterday he had sent them up a very treacherous chimney whose flue had both vertical and horizontal sections and multiple right angles. Two students had almost suffocated to death. The only sign that a logic seminar had been taking place was that Fowler had occasionally referred to the flue as "the philosophical flue."

He became, after this, quite a controversial figure. Half the university persisted in thinking him a genius, a refugee from poverty who had not only escaped his past but now wielded it as a metaphor to demolish our old beliefs about logic and language. They looked on with wonder as he crossed the quadrangle covered in soot, carrying his long adjustable rod with the brush head affixed to one end. The other half thought his escape attempt had, belatedly, failed. He was, in the end, still a chimney sweep. He was not so much wielding his past as being wielded by it, less seizing upon a metaphor than being seized upon by it, they said, and he would, in due course, cause a number of students to die of suffocation.

From our modern vantage point we understand both perspectives on Fowler. Both were right. He *did* sweep out some nineteenth-century nonsense from our understanding of logic and language, and he *did* cause the death by suffocation of numerous undergraduate and graduate students. Both were right; but these days, if Fowler is remembered at all, it's as a chimney sweep, the last of a breed, not as the first of a new kind of logician. His own body was found wedged in his own particularly narrow flue in the winter of 1953. A bricklayer had to be summoned to gain access to the corpse.

{ 4 }

THE WORKER'S FIST

· ·

In 1902 the rubber-goods mogul Moses Frenkel gave his son a large sum of money to produce the company catalog. Unbeknownst to his father, Isaac Frenkel was a nascent anarchist whose feelings toward his father—an arch-capitalist who was nevertheless a humane, compassionate man, beloved by his factory workers—were ambivalent in the extreme. Isaac embezzled the money and produced an anarchist broadsheet called *The Worker's Fist*. Isaac's ambivalent feelings, however, must have bled over into the text, for his father studied *The Worker's Fist* carefully and then congratulated him on an "outstanding rubber-goods catalog" with a "pungent, poetic title. Bravo, bravo."

{ 5 }

DIVING RECORD

....

A Florida man died Monday while trying to surpass his father's record for deep diving without the aid of oxygen or fins. Thirty years ago, in the Gulf of Mexico, the father famously dove 225 feet without using oxygen or fins. On Monday the son made three dives in the same location, all without using oxygen or fins. His first dive was 167 feet. His second dive was 191 feet. On his third attempt the son managed to dive down 216 feet without oxygen or fins, but his lungs burst on the way up and he died aboard his diving vessel. At the funeral, his father tearfully admitted that in his record-setting dive he had actually used both oxygen *and* fins.

PROGRESS

....

One of those odd accidents that so often propel scientific and technological progress. A Bavarian physicist in the first decade of the twentieth century built a brilliant apparatus intended to produce evidence to support his father's controversial theory of matter. When the evidence produced by his apparatus showed, however, that his father's theory was, on the contrary, wrong—in fact, ridiculous—he faced a choice: either demolish the apparatus, thereby obliterating all evidence of his own scientific genius, or humiliate his father.

He wandered gloomily in the mountains surrounding his lab. First he resolved to destroy the thing, to preserve his father's name by snuffing out his own. Then he resolved to do just the opposite, to thrust his apparatus into the spotlight, publish his results, make his own name by snuffing out his father's. He went back and forth between destroying his apparatus and preserving his father, and preserving his apparatus and destroying his father. He sat and stared at the apparatus with an axe in his lap, growing increasingly tormented as he pondered these equally horrifying alternatives. Then, just as his torment reached a point of unparalleled intensity and he lifted the axe high above his head, intending either to bring it down upon the apparatus (thereby preserving his father) or to fling it away from him (thereby destroying his father), he realized, all of a sudden and completely unexpectedly, that the so-called supercooled detector plate, which was actually a relatively minor component of the apparatus, could also, presumably, be used, with the proper adjustments, to *rapidly freeze meats*.

Thus modern-day meat preservation was born.

Happy ending for the world—not so much for the father and son, who later fell out over the son's frozen-beef export empire. The father could not understand how such a promising young physicist could abandon science for such a sordid and unscrupulous industry. He never found out that he had his son's flash-frozen patties to thank for the endurance of his ridiculous theory of matter, which reigned supreme until his death and was superseded only with the development of quantum mechanics in the 1920s. The son's technique, of course considerably modernized, remains to this day the most effective way to freeze beef quickly.

UNLIKE SOFIA COPPOLA

....

For his first film, the great director's son has gone to extraordinary lengths to avoid the appearance of nepotism. He did
not use a dime of his father's money. He did not use his father's
usual cast or crew. He did not use his father's film camera, or
any film camera at all, to avoid the appearance of nepotism. He
filmed everything with his eyes and stored it all in his mind,
to avoid the appearance of nepotism. Instead of using actors
and a script—his father's method—he relied heavily on regular people, going right up to them on the street and looking at
them with his huge eyes, all to avoid even a hint of nepotism.
A very *improvisational* film, to avoid the appearance of nepotism. Even though his father has an editing bay in his home, the
son has refused to use it to edit down the hours upon hours of
footage that he has stored in his mind, preferring to do it on a
specific bench he likes beside a bicycle shop. Instead of playing

the film in theaters—his father's method—he projects it onto a thirty-by-seventy-foot screen inside his mind and summarizes it for others.

As a result of these precautions, no one accuses the young director of nepotism, the way they do Sofia Coppola.

OUR SYSTEM

....

A philosopher had spent his lifetime pondering the nature of knowledge and was ready at long last to write down his conclusions. He took out a sheet of white paper and a pen. But he noticed, upon lifting the pen, a slight tremor in his hand. Hours later he was diagnosed with a neuromuscular disorder that promptly began ravaging his body, though apparently, according to the doctor, not his mind.

He lost the use of his muscles one by one: first in his fingers, then in his toes, then in his arms, then in his legs. Soon he could only whisper weakly and twitch his right eyelid. Just before losing the power of speech entirely, he designed with his son's help a system by which he could communicate, through twitches and blinks, the letters of the alphabet.

Then the philosopher fell silent.

He and his son embarked laboriously upon the writing of his book on knowledge. The father blinked or twitched his right eyelid; the son wrote down the corresponding letter. Progress was extraordinarily slow. After twenty years, they had written one hundred pages. Then, one morning, when the son picked up the pen, he noticed a slight tremor in his hand. He was diagnosed with the same neuromuscular disorder as his father—it was, naturally, hereditary—and began losing the use of his muscles, too. Soon he could only whisper weakly and manipulate his tongue. He and his own son designed a system with which he could communicate, by tapping his teeth with his tongue, the letters of the alphabet, and then he, too, fell silent.

The writing continued, though the pace, already indescribably slow, slowed even further. The grandfather blinked or twitched his right eyelid, his son tapped a tooth with his tongue, and the grandson wrote down the corresponding letter. After another twenty years, they had written another ten pages on the nature of knowledge.

One morning, the grandson noticed a slight tremor in his hand. He knew instantly what it meant. He did not even bother getting the diagnosis. His final surviving muscle was his left eyebrow, and by raising or lowering it just so he could communicate letters to his son. Again the pace slowed by an order of magnitude. The opportunities for error multiplied. Then his son was stricken, then his son's son, then his son's son's son, and then his son's son's son's son, who is my father.

We cram into our ancestral sickroom. It is dark and cold: we keep the blinds lowered and the heat down due to our hereditary light sensitivity and our hereditary heat intolerance, both of which are in fact unrelated to our hereditary neuromuscular disorder.

Someone tries to cough, but cannot. I sit at the desk and await the next letter, which can take months to arrive. The philosopher blinks or twitches his right eyelid; his son taps a tooth with his tongue; his son raises or lowers his left eyebrow; his son sucks on his upper or lower lip; his son flares a nostril; my grandfather blinks or twitches his left eyelid; my father taps a tooth with his tongue; and I write down the letter. Over the past eleven years I've written down the following:

CCCONCEPPTCCCCCAAAAACCCCCCCCCCPPC-CCCCCPCCCCCCCPCCCCCCC

What to make of this? Perhaps the philosopher has lost his mind. Perhaps there's been a disruption in our system of twitches and blinks and tooth-tapping and lip-sucking by which a letter is transmitted from his head to my pen. Perhaps—I certainly don't rule this out!—I have lost *my* mind; perhaps no matter what my father taps I see only *c*'s, and the occasional *p*. Or perhaps our system works perfectly, our philosopher's mind works perfectly, his theory of knowledge reaches the page just as he intends it, and I simply do not have the wherewithal to understand it. That, too, cannot be ruled out.

A letter is now coming my way. The old men grimace and suck, twitch and tap, blink and blow. My son, here to watch, looks on with pity and terror, still not sure how all this relates to him. He hates being in this room. You should see how eagerly at the end of the day he kisses his ancestors and races out ahead of me into the hall.

TURIN, 1962

....

Last year a Russian performance artist by the name of Pavlensky nailed his scrotum to the cobblestones of Red Square in Moscow to protest the supposed "perversity" of Russian society. From prison, he told the journal *Artforum* that he was inspired by the "absurdities of the Russian government." When asked if he was inspired by other *artists* as well, Pavlensky said no, he was inspired only by reality. What about Hedegaard? asked the appropriately skeptical *Artforum* interviewer, but Pavlensky claimed never to have heard of the important Danish scrotum-nailer, who has been nailing his scrotum to objects and surfaces for more than forty years.

Pavlensky is not the first or last artist to efface his influences, but those of us who follow contemporary art were galled that he would deny even *knowing* about Hedegaard, who just recently nailed to much acclaim his scrotum to the wing of a jumbo jet in Paris.

Eventually we were able to prove conclusively that Pavlensky did attend a 1993 exhibition in Helsinki at which Hedegaard nailed his scrotum to the hood of a car. When presented with this evidence, Pavlensky said he did not recall Hedegaard's performance, and then launched into a diversionary jeremiad against the centrality of oil money to Russian politics.

Reached by *Artforum* at his workshop in Copenhagen, where he was preparing a small piece called *Scrotum on Steel,* Hedegaard was remarkably gracious. First of all, he said, our work is very different. His is political, mine is not. Second, he said, I would not be who I am, I would not do what I do, if I had not seen Moretti staple his testicles to a fence post in Turin, 1962. We all come from somewhere, he said.

Hedegaard and Pavlensky, who was released from prison not long ago, are now rumored to be planning a joint exhibition. We do not know for certain to what they will be nailing their scrota, but they have reportedly rented a vast warehouse on the outskirts of Stuttgart.

{ 10 }

CONCERTO FOR A CORPSE

....

Probably no pianist in history has suffered as devastating a sequence of calamities as befell Pavel Hronek, the brilliant doomed Czech.

Just months after debuting to great acclaim with his father's Concerto in B Minor, Hronek lost the pinky finger of his right hand in what he described as an *eating incident* at a Prague restaurant. Critics declared his career over; Hronek himself announced his retirement. Yet less than a year later he made a glorious return with his father's Concerto for Nine Fingers.

His fame now was even greater than before. He crisscrossed the continent, played before kings and prime ministers. But in 1911, at a Parisian brasserie, he suffered another *eating incident* and lost the index finger of his left hand.

There is no coming back from this one, critics said.

"I am done!" Hronek bellowed at the journalists who crowded in the stairwell of his apartment building. "I am finished! Leave me alone!"

The very next year, of course, came his stunning performance of the Concerto for Eight Fingers, composed by his father.

Soon World War I loomed. With his mutilated hands and his cultural prestige, Hronek was clearly of more use to the Austro-Hungarian Empire in concert halls than on battlefields. Not only was he not drafted, he was actively discouraged from enlisting. But for reasons that musicologists continue to debate, Hronek insisted on joining the army anyway.

At the Battle of Galicia, one of the first of the war, Hronek's left arm was shot by a Russian sniper and had to be amputated at the elbow. His commander later recalled that Hronek kept kind of accidentally lifting both of his arms above the lip of the trench. "Hronek!" he would bark. "Keep your arms down!" And Hronek would lower his arms. But a couple of minutes later the arms would drift up above the parapet again. "Hronek!" the commander would bark. "Don't you want to play piano again?" And Hronek would say yes and lower his arms again, but only temporarily. Finally, his left arm was shot and amputated.

His father began composing the Concerto for the Right Hand almost immediately. Hronek's wartime performance of the piece with the Vienna Philharmonic is considered by many aficionados to be one of the greatest piano performances of the last century.

Days after the armistice, Hronek lost his right thumb in an *eating incident* at his apartment in Prague. The following month he lost his remaining ring finger in an *eating incident*. He told journalists he would never, under any circumstances, touch a piano again. In May he performed, before a packed concert hall, his father's Concerto for Two Fingers. Musically, it wasn't great, critics said, but as an expression of the resilience of the will it was a revelation.

Tragically, this would be the only performance of the concerto, for that summer Hronek mangled his right arm in what he called a *hunting accident*. Asked to elaborate, he said it was a *boating incident*. The arm had to be amputated at the elbow.

Hronek's father embarked on his Concerto for Two Stumps, but midway through its composition Hronek's body was found floating facedown in the River Vltava.

His father spent the last twenty years of his life composing a final piano concerto. It is believed that at least four of the era's most illustrious pianists approached him about playing it, but he told each of them that it was intended for his son.

THE FLEMISH
ENGRAVER'S SON

....

A seer whose prophecies had never failed foretold that the artistic fame of the great Flemish engraver Dierckx would one day be eclipsed by that of his infant son. Dierckx immediately built a small stone tower behind his home and locked up his son in it. The boy never learned to speak. He never learned to draw, never held an artistic tool, never encountered paint, clay, or wood. Twice a day he received through a slot in the wall a meal of bread and water, and as he ate his father watched from a peephole to ensure that nothing artistic was made of it. The boy had no medium with which to express himself; even his excretions were promptly removed. Nor, to the father, did he seem to possess an artistic sensibility at all. He ate, drank, urinated, shat. In winter he sat huddled in his rags. In summer he pressed his forehead to the cool stone floor. He moaned, he howled, he quaked. Often he dashed his head against the wall.

But none of this reassured the engraver. Just the opposite, in fact. He'd surpassed his own masters not by engraving better what they engraved well, but by engraving what they had not even thought to engrave. Likewise, the way in which his son surpassed him artistically, he would probably not even recognize as art.

Any of this might be the art! The moaning, the howling, the quaking. The art of rag-huddling, the art of pressing-against-stone. How he ate, how he shat: was it art? The head-dashing: art? What aspect of his son's evident insanity would one day be regarded as genius, while his own lucid engravings were left to rot? On the son's nineteenth birthday, the elderly engraver rushed into the stone tower, appeared before his son for the first and last time, and stabbed him to death with his largest chisel. The son's name is not recorded. Dierckx is still considered the high-water mark of late Renaissance Flemish engraving.

The seer's failed prophecy was little noticed, but it became a source of fascination and skepticism for the seer's son, an apprentice to his father. Whenever his father averred the perfect certainty of his prophecies, or regaled another dinner party with his impeccable predictions about the King's Duck, the Bookbinder's Goiter, or the French Merchant's Fortune, the son would inquire, with an air of naive curiosity, "What about the Flemish Engraver's Son?"

THE CHILDREN'S BOOK

· ·

For many years an author had been trying to write truthfully about his father, Allan, a sociologist at the University of Illinois who was gentle and generous to his students but terrifying toward his family. He abandoned one memoir manuscript after another out of fear of his father's reaction. Then—a breakthrough. He realized he could write honestly about his father by disguising him as a children's book character. Instead of "Allan," he wrote about "Al the Alligator." Instead of a sociologist, Al was an *alligator* sociologist. Instead of teaching at the University of Illinois, he taught at the *Alligator* University of *Southern* Illinois. The author felt liberated. Instead of tenure, Al had *alligator* tenure. In lieu of emotionally tormenting his wife—a grant writer for a nonprofit—he *ate* his wife, an *opossum* grant writer for a *woodland animals* nonprofit.

Now, in this new form, the whole book simply flowed out of him. It begins with Al the Alligator taking him to Florida, ostensibly to meet his grandfather—a depressive wombat with a tracheotomy hole—but really to have an affair with a Decision Sciences professor at Alligator Florida International University's School of Business. The Decision Sciences professor is a *goose*. The story ends four hundred or so pages later with a visit to Alligator Auschwitz, where Al makes him watch a horrifying documentary about the Alligator Holocaust over the protestations of their kind dog guide, who does not usually let animals under age fourteen watch it. Alligator Al screams at the dog guide in front of everyone: "The Alligator Holocaust is part of my *son's* history, too!"

The author is currently seeking a children's book publisher.

{ 13 }

OBLIGATION

....

A mountaineer's son—who had always been expected to fulfill his father's legacy by climbing the peak that had claimed his father's life—was put in touch, through a mutual friend, with the son of a sea kayaker who was likewise expected to traverse, by kayak, the ocean that had consumed his father.

The mutual friend had long wanted to introduce these two friends, one a college roommate and one a coworker. He was constantly telling the son of the sea kayaker, "I need to introduce you to the son of the mountaineer," or telling the son of the mountaineer, "You have to meet the sea kayaker's son." He was struck by the similarity of their situations: they were both short, pensive Jewish guys whose dads had died in the wilderness while attempting extreme physical feats, who both felt that they were expected to fulfill their fathers' legacies and attributed the imposition of this expectation to others when in fact they imposed it on themselves. They will either *love* each either or *hate* each other, the mutual friend told his girlfriend.

The mutual friend wrote them an email saying, basically, Sea kayaker's son, meet the mountaineer's son, mountaineer's son, meet the sea kayaker's son. I think you'll have a lot to talk about.

They met up a few days later at a wine bar suggested by the sea kayaker's son. The mountaineer's son had written that he was "happy to go wherever," expecting the sea kayaker's son to reply the same; then they would pick a place equidistant from each of them. But instead the son of the sea kayaker replied, "Cool, how about this place?" and linked to the website of a wine bar *significantly* closer to his own apartment than to the son of the mountaineer's. So by the time he got there, the son of the mountaineer was not exactly predisposed to like the son of the sea kayaker.

The conversation began haltingly, inauspiciously, with obligatory chitchat about their mutual friend. But soon they turned to the unbearable expectations that each bore through life due to the abortive undertaking of his respective adventurer father, and the conversation warmed. The son of the sea kayaker related how his father tried to cross the Pacific in a traditional Inuit kayak he'd built himself out of driftwood, animal skins, and whale fat. He drowned off the islands of Tuvalu. Completing this feat was the obligation that his son was burdened with—or rather, as his therapist put it, was the obligation that he had *chosen* to burden *himself* with. For years he had obsessively collected driftwood, animal skins, and whale fat. But he had always hated the sea—probably, he laughed, for obvious reasons—and was in no hurry to build his traditional kayak and set out into the Pacific. Neither, however, could he subdue or dispel, even with his therapist's help, the enveloping sense of obligation he felt.

"I know exactly what you mean!" cried the mountaineer's son. His father, he explained, had plunged to his death a hundred feet from the top of Gangkhar Puensum, the highest unclimbed mountain in the world. Now he had to climb it. Everyone told him: "You do *not* have to climb Gangkhar Puensum." His mom told him: "You do not have to climb Gangkhar Puensum." His therapist, who was not—they checked—the sea kayaker's son's therapist, told him: "This is an obstacle you have constructed for yourself in your own mind. No one expects you to climb Gangkhar Puensum."

The son of the sea kayaker smirked. "But of course you have to climb Gangkhar Puensum."

"Of course I have to fucking climb it!"

Laughter. Their mutual friend was right: they had a lot in common. Each understood the sense of obligation—half-invented and half-real, or wholly invented and at the same time wholly real, completely subjective but completely objective, ridiculous but binding—felt by the other. In many respects they were the same person, except that the sea kayaker's son hated the sea and loved the mountains, whereas the mountaineer's son hated the mountains and loved the sea. (They agreed that the sea evoked the infinite, but disagreed about whether the infinite was a good thing or a bad thing.)

They got drunker and drunker, laughed louder and louder, and at one point in the evening even cried a little bit. Sometime after midnight, the son of the sea kayaker said: "Have you ever seen *Strangers on a Train*?"

"The Hitchcock movie? I've read a plot synopsis."

"I think we should each agree to fulfill the *other's* father's legacy."

It was not a crazy idea, they realized. They shook on it. The mountaineer's son would construct a traditional Inuit kayak out of driftwood, animal skins, and whale fat, and use it to cross the Pacific. The sea kayaker's son would climb Gangkhar Puensum.

Beautiful.

Each slept uncharacteristically well that night, pleased that his father's legacy would finally be fulfilled, relieved that it would not be by him.

Their mutual friend emailed them the next morning with a new complication.

Sea kayaker's son, mountaineer's son, he wrote, meet the son of the guy who attempted the world's highest skydive. I'm sure you guys will hit it off.

They have since coordinated a three-way exchange. The mountaineer's son will cross the Pacific in a traditional Inuit kayak. The skydiver's son will summit Gangkhar Puensum. And the sea kayaker's son will leap from a balloon at 130,000 feet wearing a special pressurized suit. Each will ensure that his father's legacy is fulfilled, but without merely following in his father's footsteps. Each will at the same time honor his dad and strike out in a new, literally a new, direction from him—the mountaineer's son moving across rather than up, the skydiver's son up rather than down, and the sea kayaker's son down rather than across. It is unlikely that all three will survive their respective feats.

Their mutual friend has taken pride in orchestrating all this. His father was also known as a *great connector of people* and *facilitator of conversations* who was always *putting interesting people in a room together*.

HOSTAGE SITUATION

....

The father of a Tunisian activist kidnapped last week by extremists in Tunis has offered himself up in exchange for his son. The fathers of the extremists have offered to replace the extremists, and the fathers of the journalists covering the situation have offered to replace the journalists. The fathers of Tunisian officials have offered to replace the officials, and the fathers of Tunisian military commanders have offered to replace the commanders. Across Tunisia, the fathers of everyday Tunisians have offered to replace their sons, and, in solidarity with them, fathers around the world have offered to replace their sons. These offers, which would not solve the situation but merely age it by roughly thirty years, have been uniformly rejected.

{ 15 }

THE SWEEPER

....

A sweeper for the Canadian national curling team lost his father just one week before the 1998 Nagano Olympics. The sweeper— whose job it is to influence the path and speed of the curling stone by sweeping the ice in front of it with a broom—told his coach that he could not compete. The Canadian coach tried to respond, "I think your father would want you to keep sweeping," but apparently he found this sentence too preposterous to actually utter aloud. Three times he tried to say the sentence, "I think your father would want you to keep sweeping," but each time he found it too preposterous to utter aloud, so at the last minute the Canadians were forced to replace the sweeper with a substitute.

HERB'S PLACE

....

A man who studied the human mind through biochemistry and his son who studied it through introspection found that they had less and less to say to each other until one Christmas dinner they sat across from each other for two hours and said nothing at all.

"This is no good," said the father after dessert.

"No," said the son.

They were both sentimental men, and were both, at this point, holding back tears, though of course the father thought he was crying for fundamentally biochemical reasons while the son thought he was crying for irreducibly introspective ones.

So they came up with a plan. Each would suggest ten books to the other, books that epitomized his own worldview, respectively biochemical and introspective. They would read all ten books over the course of the year, and by next Christmas they would each understand the other's worldview and have plenty to talk about.

In January, as each energetically compiled his list, they had high hopes.

In February they traded lists. By March all the books were in hand.

But when the son opened the first book recommended by his father and read the first sentence, up to the first comma, he realized he would never understand his father's worldview. One *introspective* tear fell onto the page. Same for the father: he opened the first book, read the first clause of the first sentence, gave up on the possibility of ever understanding his son, and shed a single *biochemical* tear onto the page.

The son threw his father's books in a dumpster, and the father jammed his son's books into a charity drop box. Through an astonishing and amusing sequence of events, too illogical and unlikely to relate here, all twenty books ended up several years later at the same insane asylum library in Wisconsin, where they were discovered in two stacks of ten by an ingenious psychopath named Herbert.

Herbert read the books with great interest and incredible intensity. It was clear to him that all twenty books said exactly the same thing. One stack restated the other stack. No twenty books, Herbert felt, had ever been so akin, so harmonious, so complementary as these twenty books. He wrote down his conclusions in a four-thousand-page document, using unfortunately a grammatical system of his own invention. No publisher, needless to say, took more than one glance at the manuscript. Herbert has since published it on his blog, Herb's Place, at herbsplace.blogspot.com.

It seems unlikely that the father or son—who actually no longer speak—will ever come upon Herbert's Blogspot site, and even if they did, I doubt they would recognize it as the meeting point of their minds.

{ 17 }

NO

....

A hedge fund manager shot himself dead on the traffic island at the center of our town rotary. A subsequent examination of his finances found that this once-affluent man had gone bankrupt. It seems that he'd squandered his fortune on a series of failed films and fashion ventures by his son, a failed filmmaker, and his daughter, a failed fashion mogul. His wealth had seemed inexhaustible, but after only four of his son's terrible films and five of his daughter's profoundly misguided fashion ventures, it was all gone.

A suicide note taped to his chest read: *I tried to make you happy. —Dad.*

The son and daughter spoke to a reporter. "He never knew how to say *no* to us," said the daughter. "He should have said *no* to my films and *no* to her fashion ventures," said the son.

{ 18 }

THE DEATH OF
INSPECTOR PIRENNE

....

A 1977 profile in *Le Figaro* revealed that the Belgian author who, under the pseudonym Philippe Plateau, had created the enormously popular Inspector Pirenne novels was also responsible, under the pseudonym Ingrid Nève, for the similarly beloved erotic romance novels centering on the insatiable florist Gisèle Simonet. This revelation, combined with another in the same article—that the author was dying—threw his two readerships into a panic, a panic eased only by the rumor that the author's son, already established as a novelist in his own right, was poised to take over and carry on with both series, the crime and the erotic romance.

The origins of this rumor, much less the truth of it, were unknown. Some said that the son, eager to inherit the two lucrative franchises, had started it, but that the father was reluctant, either because he didn't want to let go of his characters or because he didn't want to burden his son with them. Others believed it was the father, anxious to see his characters live on and for his son to profit from them, who had started the rumor, and the son who was reluctant to take possession.

In any event, either the father or the son, or both, must have declined the handoff, and seemingly at the last minute, for on the final page of the last Inspector Pirenne novel, which came out months after the author was buried, crime devotees were stunned to read that their cherished Pirenne, who'd survived so many close calls, strolled out of his office one day "in high spirits," stepped on "something," and "exploded irreversibly." Romantic-erotica fanatics were similarly stunned to read that their darling Gisèle, fresh off a vigorous tryst with a young theology student, strolled out of her flower shop one evening, stepped on "something, like a mine or something," and "permanently exploded." Whether these lines were written by the author or inserted after his death by his son remains, to the one or perhaps two scholars still interested in the question, a mystery.

The son, who died himself just a couple of days ago, went on to write some extremely original poetry that attracted extraordinarily few readers. No one, as it happens, reads the Pirenne or Gisèle novels anymore, either. They aged poorly and have fallen, for the most part, out of print.

THE SULFUR BATHS

·······················

A very promising career was cut short in 1837 when one of Russia's finest young poets, on whose lungs an ominous black spot had been found, traveled to Tiflis per the urgent recommendation of his doctor to soak in the sulfur baths there. He left Moscow in May. That summer his spirits soared, the Caucasus agreed with him, his lungs, as he wrote to his father, a high-ranking military officer, "suddenly remembered what it is to *breathe*." Each morning he soaked for precisely forty-five minutes in the scalding baths and each afternoon he hiked in the hills ringing Tiflis, sketching landscapes and writing many of his most memorable verses. In August, however, his father—jubilant at his sickly son's rapid convalescence—took a monthlong leave to visit him in the Caucasus. We do not know exactly what transpired during the visit, but we can deduce that the father and son sat together in the sulfur baths at least once, an experience that evidently perturbed the young poet, since thereafter his poems—formerly filled with the most extravagant array of imagery this side of

Gogol—feature just a single image, of a fat Russian colonel delicately lowering his large genitalia into the sulfur baths of Tiflis. From September 1837 until his untimely death at Sevastopol (1855), the once-promising poet returned again and again to the seconds just before, and just after, his gingerly squatting father's big genitalia touched the steaming surface of the Tiflis sulfur baths—*to the exclusion of every other possible poetic theme.*

The poet, as one biographer correctly notes, did make an effort to conceal, or vary, the nature of his fixation, referring in some poems to the "genitals of the Muscovite lieutenant," in others to the "Russian captain's cock," here to the "testicles of a foreign adjutant," there to the "northern brigadier general's balls." But these minor variations were merely the poet rattling the bars of his obsession; he remained trapped by it. We see this perhaps most poignantly in an 1838 poem that begins, promisingly, with a charming description of a Dagestani shepherd leading his flock over a high mountain pass, follows the shepherd, worrisomely, to an alpine lake, and concludes, inevitably, with the abrupt appearance of "an old cavalry officer from Nizhny Novgorod" crouched "naked on his haunches" in the shallows of the lake, lowering his genitals "into the cold, clear water." The poet returned to Russia that year, completely recovered, but his new preoccupation returned with him. "The black spot," as the biographer puts it, a little melodramatically, "had migrated from the lungs to the poems." His star fell very, very quickly. Not he but Lermontov—with whom he had actually overlapped briefly in Tiflis but whose father, notably, had never come to visit—was now considered Pushkin's heir.

It is true that in the twentieth century there were intermittent attempts to reclaim the later work. In his *Lectures on Russian Literature*, Nabokov mentions, with partial approval, "all those old officers dipping their manhoods into all those limpid lakes and sulfurous tubs." He actually preferred these "bathetic bath scenes" to the poet's earlier "sterile vistas." Brodsky (in a forward for some reason to a book by Kiš) also hails the genital poems. But these are exceptions.

20

LAST LINE

. . . .

A historian had spent forty years on his magnum opus, a thousand-page inquiry into the origins of the Jewish joke, when he died of an aneurysm. His son found him at his desk, slumped over his manuscript, which was lacking only a last line.

Determined to honor his beloved father by completing his book, the son tried to think of a fitting final sentence. He put one down, but then erased it. It wasn't right.

He wrote down another last line, but erased that one, too.

And then another.

And another.

All at once, the son felt the huge weight of his task. Not only did this last sentence have to follow logically from the second-to-last; not only did it have to conclude the final chapter and the entire book in a satisfying way; not only did it have to remain stylistically consistent with what came before; it also had to be worthy of his father's prose, worthy of his principles, worthy of his intellect—worthy of his *life*.

Yes, this last line had to do justice to his father's whole life and life's work! To vindicate it! To redeem it!

He felt it hovering there just out of reach, a last line that would consummate his father's book. The son groped after this perfect last line for a month. Then a year. Then ten years. Finally forty years had gone by without his having written a word and he, too, died of an aneurysm at his desk.

He was discovered by his son, who now read for the first time his grandfather's manuscript. What his father had interpreted as the second-to-last line, he realized, was clearly intended to be the last line. Adding another would be redundant and ridiculous. The book was complete. But it was now outmoded, obsolete, even embarrassing, so to preserve his family's good name he consigned it to the flames.

To this day, though, the grandson can still recall the powerful last line of his grandfather's manuscript. The finality of it is apparently *overwhelming*.

21

IN EQUILIBRIUM

....

For twenty-two generations, the Auerbach family had oscillated extremely effectively between men of action and men of thought. The men of action set sail and set interest rates, moralized and legislated, built buildings and drew borders. Their sons, appalled by the frenetic, hypocritical, impermanent, and ultimately meaningless lives of their fathers, became men of thought, each eventually producing one *monumental biography* of his father and one *obviously autobiographical novel* about father-son relationships. Their sons, in turn, were appalled by their feeble, self-conscious fathers, etiolated and articulate, paralyzingly consistent in their thinking, nonsexual, sitting for fifty or sixty years in their studies with words on the tips of their tongues. They became men of action.

There had been eleven Auerbach buildings and eleven Auerbach biographies, eleven interest rate policies and eleven obviously autobiographical novels about fathers and sons. A system in equilibrium, regular as a pendulum.

But now, in the twenty-third generation, the whole thing has fallen out of kilter: a man of thought has reared, inexplicably, another man of thought. That spells the end. A family might be able to withstand two consecutive men of action, but two consecutive men of thought, meaning two consecutive novels on the same theme, both obviously autobiographical, as well as a biography about a biographer: no system can endure that much uninterrupted introspection.

{ 22 }

HAND-ME-DOWNS

....

Only hours after the funeral, his very frugal sister had called to see if he wanted a "completely unopened" stick of deodorant she had found in their father's bathroom, and knowing that she was not the sort of person for whom *because it's my dead dad's* would constitute a sufficient reason for turning down a perfectly usable stick of deodorant, still wearing, as she confirmed in response to his initial query, its plastic skullcap underneath its outer shell, he had regretfully explained that he used neither the father's brand, Speed Stick, nor the father's scent, Ultimate Sport.

As it happens, the completely unopened stick of deodorant did not go to waste: it was ultimately made use of by the sister's pliable husband, the movie-quoting digital marketing manager, who, the son observed, soon started to smell just like his dead father, the marketing manager's father-in-law.

Before long, the brother-in-law was also wearing the dead man's "basically brand new" winter jacket and his "almost un-worn" sneakers—both of which, the son had to admit, his sister had offered to him first, and which he had declined for good reasons, but which were nonetheless disturbing to see ornamenting this digital marketing professional and movie aficionado's chest and feet.

Then, just as he was growing accustomed to his brother-in-law wearing his father's deodorant, winter jacket, and sneakers, the son noticed that he'd begun wearing his dead father's personality and philosophy. The son first observed this during a recent family dinner at Empire Szechuan, at which his brother-in-law not only smelled like his father under the armpits and looked like him around the chest and feet but also sounded like him out of the mouth. Evidently his sister had scrounged around not only in their father's bathroom and closet, but also in his head. In his bathroom she'd found perfectly usable deodorant, in his closet she'd found perfectly usable jackets and shoes, and in his head she'd found perfectly usable traits, tastes, and ideas.

The son turned down the deodorant, jacket, and shoes, and long ago had politely declined the traits, tastes, and ideas, but the son-in-law was willing to wear whatever his wife threw at him. They had evidently stood beside the father's head, the sister reaching in for this or that emotional tendency or political belief, her husband trying it on. If it fit, great, he took it! If it didn't, no problem, back it went in the father's head, and then with the head to the grave. Presumably the brother-in-law was under no obligation to *like* any of these traits, tastes, and ideas, but evidently he *had* liked a lot of them, or liked that his wife liked them, because he was wearing so many of them that evening at Empire Szechuan, in addition to the family deodorant (which, it should be said, *was*, in fact, the son's brand, and had been ever since his father had purchased for him his early pubertal equipment many years before.)

The son waited till his brother-in-law went to the bathroom before accusing his thrifty sister of ransacking their father's head for these "intellectual, psychological, and emotional hand-me-downs." But she claimed not to know what he was talking about.

ACCEPTED DONATIONS

....

A different son faced a similar quandary following his father's death. It was easy enough to divide his father's money and material things among him and his brothers. But what about his father's mental things? His quirks, temper, and jokes? His optimism, nostalgia, sentimentality, and rigor? His binaries, concepts, and explanatory frameworks? His idea of what constituted worthwhile work? His areas of interest? His blind spots?

The son certainly didn't want them. But he didn't want his brothers to have them, either. And he didn't want them just to disappear with their father. They were worth preserving, but he honestly *did not have room* for them in his head, and he didn't think it was fair for his brothers to take them if he couldn't (even though they said they would be happy to).

Finally the son looked into charities: Goodwill, the Salvation Army. But most of the major American charities, he discovered, accept only financial or material donations, not immaterial or conceptual ones. The Salvation Army accepts secondhand clothing or household items, but not secondhand ideas, theoretical approaches, or psychological attitudes. This actually prompted a screaming match with a Salvation Army officer who conceded that many of his father's mental things—his commitment, his self-confidence, his faculties of concentration—might very well be more useful to a poor person than his material things, but still wouldn't budge on the Salvation Army policy regarding tangibility.

A policeman later caught him trying to stuff his father's admirably pragmatic attitude toward death and life into a Goodwill donation box. Dispositions, the son pointed out, were not featured on the list of unacceptable items. It is not a hazardous chemical, he said. It's not paint, solvent, or oil. It's not a mattress! It's not a box spring! It is an *outlook* or *standpoint*. Not unkindly, the policeman showed him that while standpoints did not appear on the list of unacceptable items, nor were they on the list of accepted items. Why, asked the policeman, not unkindly, if it's so good, don't you want to keep it for yourself? Or is that getting into complicated territory? And the son said, Yeah, kind of getting into complicated territory there.

Happily, the son did find, eventually, a small charity that would accept discarded mental attributes. They took everything of the father's apart from his *arachnophobia* and his *love of family*—both of which they had in surplus—and his *moral righteousness*, which was unusual but too idiosyncratic, they said, to find a good home for. Surprisingly, they were willing to take his *casual interest in jazz,* his *elementary knowledge of military history,* his *feelings about small dogs versus big dogs,* his *impatience with organizations,* his *disdain for metaphysics,* and even his *vague childhood memory of visit to unidentified lake.* Apparently there is now a village in the West African Sahel whose residents have been able to put his father's mental things to good use. The charity does a really nice job. Once a year the son gets an update about the villagers: Mariam has taken out a microloan with the aid of your father's *numeracy.* Ibrahima has started a small crafts business using your father's *self-confidence.* Youssouf is now planning to become a soil scientist thanks to your father's *idea of what constitutes worthwhile work.*

{ 24 }

THE FURNITURE STORE OWNER'S SON

....

In Vilnius, around the turn of the twentieth century, an assimilated Jewish businessman who owned a thriving furniture store was stunned and profoundly disturbed to learn that his relationship with his son, which was tense in the usual ways but by no means unloving, had been converted—by the son—into a theory of history, society, eschatology, art, the novel, and politics. This was, of course, the period during which artistic and intellectual Jews all across Europe were busily converting the particulars of their relationships with their recently assimilated businessman fathers into art of supposedly universal significance and ideas of supposedly universal application. But the furniture store owner was unfamiliar with these works. When he came across his son's book, in which he and his sofas, beds, and hardwood chairs and his (always well-meaning) efforts to introduce his son to the furniture trade were made to represent more or less the whole

cosmos, the march of human history, and the form of the bour-
geois novel, he was devastated.

He summoned his son to the furniture store.

"Is this," he asked, holding up the book, which he had hardly
understood, "really what you think of me?"

Yet the son was already transposing the particulars of *this*
conversation, their last of any substance, into a universal key.

TWO HATS

· ·

The son of the late philosopher-mystic Perelmann, who was writing a biography of his father, used to say at our weekly brown bag colloquiums that he wore two hats: that of Perelmann's son and that of his biographer. We assumed that this was just a figure of speech until a graduate student who happened to be renting an apartment across the street from him reported that he really wore two *physical hats*: the son-of-Perelmann hat was a Boston Red Sox cap and the biographer-of-Perelmann hat was a brown fedora. Some evenings he wore the Red Sox cap, some evenings he wore the brown fedora, and some evenings he went back and forth, more or less rapidly, between the cap and the fedora.

Word circulated, and before long the chair of the department knocked on Perelmann's son's office door. The chair urged him to take some time off, please, for his own sake.

"Bill," said Perelmann's son with a knowing smile. "Is this about the hats?"

The chair admitted that he was concerned.

"Bill," said Perelmann's son again, touching the chair's wrist. "Don't worry about me. I'm not going crazy, at least not yet! The hats serve a purely functional purpose."

It looked silly, he knew, but the hats helped him keep separate his two conflicting roles—first as a son still grieving for his dad, second as a scholar trying to understand, to historicize, and, yes, to critique, as dispassionately as possible, his father's ideas. Before hitting upon the two-hat system, he'd lived in a state of perpetual self-reproach: when he thought of Perelmann the way a son thinks of his dad, the scholar in him condemned his lack of objectivity, and when he thought of Perelmann the way a scholar thinks of his subject, the son in him condemned his lack of loyalty.

The hats put an end to all that.

When he pulled on the old Red Sox cap, its snug fit and familiar smell had a Proustian effect. He was returned to the grandstands of Fenway Park, beside his father. He was suffused with compassion and pity, with respect, love, and acceptance—for his father's flaws no less than for his virtues. He wanted to annihilate his father's academic detractors and slaughter those who would attempt to understand him as a product of his milieu. Such was the effect of the Red Sox cap. But under the weight of the brown fedora, beneath its sober brim, he could put aside his childish devotion and scrutinize his father's thought with the skepticism required of an intellectual historian. He investigated the genealogy of his father's ideas, examined their internal consistency, considered their presuppositions and limitations.

"Bill, I admit it's a strange system!" said Perelmann's son, laughing. "That what happens *in* our heads should be so affected by what happens *on top* of our heads. But for me, this does seem to be the case." He shrugged. "It helps me proceed. I do not question it."

The department chair went away intensely impressed, even moved. Word went forth that Perelmann's son was not crazy, but brilliant.

At our next brown bag colloquium, Perelmann's son claimed to wear "four hats." He was Perelmann's son, Perelmann's biographer, Perelmann's philosophical interlocutor, and Perelmann's estate executor.

The next morning the graduate student reported that two new hats, a black bowler and a purple yarmulke, had entered the rotation. From what he'd seen, he hypothesized that the bowler was the executor hat and the yarmulke was the interlocutor hat. Perelmann's son had spent most of the early evening going calmly back and forth between the Red Sox cap and the bowler. At around eight o'clock the yarmulke went on and stayed on until just after nine. From then until midnight, he frantically switched between the yarmulke, the Red Sox cap, and the brown fedora. He ended the night with forty-five relatively relaxed minutes in the black bowler.

"I'm fine, Bill!" said Perelmann's son, touching the chair's wrist. "How can I summon memories of my father one minute, and deal with his taxes the next? Impossible, unless I *physically put on the bowler hat*. One minute I'm recalling the sensation of being up on his shoulders, the next I'm attacking his peculiar interpretation of Kant? *The purple yarmulke*. Who taught him this idiosyncratic Kant, and when? *Brown fedora*."

By the next colloquium, Perelmann's son wore sixteen hats. He was Perelmann's son, Perelmann's biographer, Perelmann's philosophical interlocutor, Perelmann's estate executor, Perelmann's publicist, Perelmann's usurper, Perelmann's housekeeper, Perelmann's zealot, Perelmann's annihilator, Perelmann's designated philosophical heir, Perelmann's defector, Perelmann's librarian, Perelmann's gene carrier, Perelmann's foot soldier, Perelmann's betrayer, and Perelmann's doppelgänger. Twelve new hats joined the repertoire, including a beret, a bandana, a small straw hat, and a sombrero.

Naturally, we were a little alarmed. His evenings, the graduate student reported, were now mere blurs of hat transitions. Nothing stayed on his head for long. But reality, we assumed, would sooner or later impose a limit on his mania. There are only so many kinds of hats, just as there are only so many relations that can possibly obtain between a father and a son. In due course Perelmann's son would run out of either hats or relations, we thought—probably hats—and thereafter he would return to reason.

But soon there were relations we had never considered, hats we'd never heard of. He was Perelmann's old–Jewish–joke repository, Perelmann's voice impersonator, Perelmann's sweater-wearer, the last living practitioner of Perelmann's skiing technique, Perelmann's surpasser, Perelmann's victim. He wore an eighteenth-century tricorne, a deerstalker, a round Hasidic kolpik, an Afghan pakol with a peacock feather tucked into its folds.

By the end of fall semester we knew something had to be done. The explosion of hats and relations had not abated. Left alone, we realized, Perelmann's son would partition his relationship with his father ad infinitum, and for each infinitesimal slice of relationship he would purchase a hat. Ultimately he would turn his relationship with his father—by nature, one simple thing—into something infinitely complex, and his hat collection would, correspondingly, grow without bound, and he would wind up destroying himself. His analytical tendency, along with the huge hat collection that resulted from it, would obliterate him.

So, one morning, in an attempt to save him from himself, a group of graduate students and junior faculty members slipped, with the department chair's blessing, into Perelmann's son's apartment. (He was at a Perelmann conference.) We gathered all the hats and put them in garbage bags—128 hats in twelve garbage bags—and got them out of there.

But in our hearts we must have known that we were treating the symptom, not the cause. Yesterday, according to our informant, Perelmann's son spent all day and all night in a ten-gallon hat of thus far unknown paternal associations.

{ 26 }

DEAD LANGUAGE

....

Linguists last year were overjoyed to discover two living speakers, a father and son, of a Finnic language long believed to be extinct. The father lived in North Karelia, the son in South Karelia. Both agreed to be flown to Helsinki to have a conversation observed and recorded by a consortium of eighty linguists in the hope of preserving the language. But the conversation was so stilted, so perfunctory, so silence-ridden and self-conscious that afterward the eighty linguists declared the language, for all intents and purposes, extinct. This is said to be the first time a language has ever been declared extinct while there are still people alive who speak it.

{ 27 }

THE CLOCK TOWER

....

A familiar legend—recounted, for example, by the Czech folk-lorist František Neff—has it that the clockmaker behind Prague's remarkable astronomical clock, which ticks away to this day in the Old Town Square, the figure of Death striking every hour, had his eyes plucked out by the Councillors of Prague so that he could never repeat his work, much less surpass it.

Now, the clockmaker had three sons, the eldest of whom was an expert horologist in his own right. He planned to avenge his father, to whom he was exceptionally devoted, by constructing in a little Bohemian village an even more spectacular astronomical clock, twice as tall, twice as ornate, and twice as accurate as the clock in Prague. He worked, of necessity, in total secrecy. But as the clock tower grew in height the secret became harder to contain. When it finally came out, the Councillors of Prague marched on the village, knocked down the tower, arrested the eldest son, and plucked out his eyes.

The clockmaker's middle son was a competent horologist, and moderately devoted to his father. He also—as he told his older brother—was rational, and valued his eyes. He was reluctant to do what his brother, with his appallingly empty sockets, asked of him: to build, in a remote Moravian village, an astronomical clock three times as tall, three times as ornate, and three times as accurate as the Prague clock, in order to avenge their father and humiliate the Councillors of Prague. But his older brother, besides being an expert horologist and a devoted son, was an indefatigable requester of things, and a skilled instiller of guilt. "After everything Dad's done for us," he said, "this is the least we could do for him. I would do it myself, but as you know the Councillors plucked out my eyes." (He pointed manipulatively at his sockets.) At last the middle son was worn down. He began building a wondrous clock tower in an obscure corner of Moravia, far from Prague's scrutiny, but word reached the Councillors of Prague nevertheless. They marched over, knocked down the clock tower, and plucked out the middle son's eyes.

The clockmaker's youngest son was a poor horologist, and not particularly devoted to his father. Yet here, as in a nightmare, came his oldest brother with his empty sockets and his "suggestion"—it always began as a mere suggestion—that his little brother build a clock tower four times taller, four times more ornate, and four times more accurate than their father's clock tower, for the purposes of vengeance, but with the inevitable result (as the youngest pointed out) that the Councillors of Prague would knock it down and pluck out his eyes.

Life became miserable for the youngest son. All day long he

took care of the three blind horologists, who chattered about clocks or hurled imprecations at the Councillors of Prague; periodically his oldest brother took him aside and muttered significantly about family and duty and "suggested" he construct a clock tower four times better than the one in Prague; meanwhile a rumor circulated that the Councillors were coming for his eyes as a kind of preventive measure. He could not understand how this had become his life; *he was not even interested in timekeeping.*

Finally, one day, he disappeared.

František Neff, the folklorist, traces two variants of the legend. In one, the youngest son was seized by the Councillors of Prague, his eyes plucked out and his head put on a spike that emerges, briefly, to music, from his father's clock every autumnal equinox. In the other variant, told mostly to children, he escaped to the mountains, where he is, even now, building a clock tower that will eventually surpass Prague's in every dimension.

COMMENTARY

....

For more than nine hundred years, a line of sages in a remote region of Hokkaido, Japan, has produced commentary after commentary on an ancient text of ethical and metaphysical reflection that was lost long ago. Each commentary serves as the primary source for the commentary that succeeds it.

By the fourteenth century it had struck one sage that the chain of commentary was generating ethical and metaphysical questions rather than answers, obscurity rather than clarity, sadness rather than happiness. This is what he wrote in his commentary, a call to end all commentary, a text which became known as the *Cessation Commentary*.

His successor studied this commentary carefully and responded with a stack of blank paper: a refusal, based on the wisdom of his predecessor, to comment at all. The stack of paper became known as the *Blank Commentary*.

His successor, the sage Taku, observed that a blank commentary is still a commentary. It parodied commentary, it abjured commentary, but that was, of course, a commentary of its own. Taku wrote this observation on a piece of paper and then burned himself alive with it, bellowing as the flames incinerated him that he had no commentary of his own to pass on. This is alternatively known as the *Fire Commentary* or the *No-Commentary Commentary*.

By now it was becoming clear that the process of ending all commentary would be harder for this little Hokkaido sect than it had originally assumed.

Taku's successor moved to a big city and sold noodles on the street (*The Noodle-Banality Commentary*). His successor destroyed the sect's temple and its archive of past commentaries (*The Obliteration Commentary*). His successor was the famed sage Ozaki. Ozaki waited for his own successor to come of age, captured him, gagged his mouth and bound his wrists, locked him in a trunk, and drowned him in the Sea of Okhotsk. For the rest of his life Ozaki roamed the streets of the village with a long sword and a vow to cut the head off any man who interpreted what he had done as a commentary. When he died, his brother told the few villagers who attended his funeral that Ozaki was really a decent and gentle soul who'd adopted this fearsome persona purely to emancipate the sect from the ruinous chain of commentary that had gripped it for so long. This eulogy became known as the *Justification Commentary*, and Ozaki's actions were retrospectively called the *Emancipation Commentary*.

Recent sages have tried alcohol, drugs, and sex. They have pursued normalcy, or silence, or madness. They have published good and bad poetry. Three went into politics, two into finance, two into tech, and one moved to Minneapolis–Saint Paul and was never heard from again (*The Twin Cities Disappearance Commentary*). Still, in spite of their efforts, the tradition of commentary persists. Incidentally, a theologian in Tübingen who is an authority on the sect recently published a paper suggesting that the original ethico-metaphysical text may never have existed in the first place.

{ 29 }

EXPLANATION

. . . .

A philosopher famous for his gnomic aphorisms was found stabbed to death in his Paris apartment. Beside the body his aphorisms were found explained to death. His son, a proponent of clear thinking and clear writing, has confessed to stabbing his father, whom he called an obscurantist, and explaining his aphorisms, in both cases to death. According to Paris police, the son stabbed his father eleven times in the back and then typed up long, lucid explanations of each of his aphorisms. An erudite coroner pronounced both the father and his aphorisms dead at the scene.

{ 30 }

VINDICATED

....

A father's fears were vindicated in the worst possible way when his only son—whom he had always admonished for "eating too quickly"—choked to death on a salmon roll at a New York sushi bar. The father immediately set to work on a eulogy. Observing the zeal with which he set about this terrible task, his wife became concerned. Her concerns were vindicated in the worst way when he delivered, to a packed synagogue, a eulogy entitled: "My Son, the Speed Eater."

{ 31 }

IN THE HOUSE OF THE CRYPTOPORTICUS

. . . .

Although the plaster casts of Pompeii's dead, buried alive in the ash of Mount Vesuvius, have furnished archaeologists with a wealth of knowledge about the lives and customs of Roman citizens, one particular pair of immaculately preserved corpses, caught in the extremely narrow underground passageway of the so-called House of the Cryptoporticus, and identified by a consensus of scientists as a father and a son, has inspired only endless debate. Were the father and son trying to squeeze past one another, as some archaeologists believe? Or, as others maintain, was this some sort of embrace, something between a handshake and a hug? The infighting in the latter camp has been, if possible, even more vicious, with one faction deducing from a careful analysis of the arms that the father was initiating a hug while the son countered with a handshake, and another faction, from its own thorough arms analysis, fervently committed to the position that the *son* was actually going in for the hug while the *father* reciprocated with a handshake, perhaps anticipating—some in this faction theorize—that the son would find a hug awkward, not realizing—they believe—that the eruption, the prospect of imminent death, had in a sense annulled the old conventions between them and made the son want, quite simply, to hug his father. Yet another contingent, a splinter group of this second faction, agrees that the son here is going for the hug and the father for the handshake, but claims to see signs that if the ash had caught them a moment earlier we would have seen the reverse: father going for the hug, son going for the handshake. The embarrassing failure of *that* embrace caused each party, these archaeologists contend, to abruptly and clumsily adopt the other's strategy—i.e., handshake for father, hug for son—and this just happened to be the position they were in when the burning ash buried them and they were immortalized.

Giuseppe Fiorelli, the astute Italian archaeologist who produced their plaster casts in 1863, was, incidentally, one of those who believed the two figures were simply trying to squeeze past one another, in order to escape from the House of the Cryptoporticus. He was not even convinced the two were related, or that they were men.

{ 32 }

IN A VAT

. . . .

At an upscale Italian café on the Upper West Side, a father found himself in the peculiar position of trying to persuade his son that some things could be known with certainty, beyond a shadow of a doubt, and he gave as an example the fact that they were right now drinking cappuccinos together at an Italian café on Columbus Avenue, near Eighty-Third Street. That's something that we can both know with certainty, said the father—a starting point for us. But the son refused to admit even *this* much, since one, or both, of them might be a brain in a vat. Even after his father had paid for the (expensive) cappuccinos, the son would not admit that they had necessarily drunk anything together, much less cappuccinos, since either of them, or both of them, might be in vats, he said, and they left the café in silence.

It so happens that the son's skepticism is not unwarranted: he actually *is* a brain suspended in a vat, tended to by a scientist who feeds it electrical impulses that conjure up whole illusory worlds. The father-son conversation just reported, which supposedly took place at Tarallucci e Vino on Columbus and Eighty-Third, really occurred solely within the synapses of the son's floating brain. The scientist keyed in "philosophical debate about the possibility of knowledge" and "rustic, refined Italian café," and voilà.

Next, the scientist keyed in "cathartic embrace" and "unpretentious clam shack" and "southern Maine" and the son's brain believed he was hugging his father in Kittery.

The really sad thing—besides, I suppose, the delusions, dimly surmised, of this disembodied brain—is that the mad scientist's father, himself a retired physician, lives literally right around the corner, yet they hardly see each other at all. The father believes that his son is conducting all kinds of important brain experiments and has no interest in hanging out with his old man. He would be surprised—this is putting it mildly—to learn that his son actually uses his brain-in-a-vat to simulate thousands of encounters between fathers and sons, in every possible permutation. Why the mad scientist would rather simulate these father-son encounters than experience them firsthand is an open question, one that he's currently trying to answer through his simulations.

{ 33 }

DIVERGENCE FROM LESCANNE

....

An admirer of the avant-garde French sculptor Lescanne modeled his life after his idol's. He wore bright teal socks like Lescanne did, smoked hashish like Lescanne did, and sent his children off to live with his older sister just like Lescanne did a hundred years before. But whereas Lescanne had accidentally murdered his wife during a game of William Tell by shooting her in the face, his admirer successfully shot the apple off his wife's head. The admirer's wife was unwilling to try the game again.

The admirer has since stopped sculpting. He still wears the socks and smokes the drugs, but the continued existence of his wife, a preschool teacher, is now a constant reminder of the degree to which he has diverged from his idol.

{ 34 }

ICE CLIMBERS

....

On the twentieth anniversary of his father's disappearance during an ice climbing expedition, a son flew to Banff National Park in hopes of finding, at last, his father's body. He was not, it turned out, the only one with that idea: on this bright spring day the park was virtually overrun with sons searching for their vanished fathers, each of whom had fallen through one crevasse or another. There was a kind of festival atmosphere. Every now and then a cry went up as another son found his preternaturally well-preserved father, still wearing, in almost every case, his helmet, his harness, and his crampons.

The son in question did not find his father, but the experience was nevertheless life-changing, like his Israel trip after sophomore year. There was something sort of holy about this search for these long-gone ice-climbing fathers, who—it escaped no one—had all, at one point, kissed their young sons good-bye to go scamper up a waterfall. The sons were all in this together. Everyone pitched in. There was no competition whatsoever, no rivalry, just sons helping sons break up these great big slabs of ice with specialized ice picks to see if their fathers were inside. Breaking apart an ice slab and finding a perfectly preserved ice-climbing father inside felt good regardless of whether it was your friend's father or your own or the father of some guy you'd just met.

He went back the next year, and the year after, and the year after that. He didn't find his father's body, but in the sons of these missing ice climbers he found a community. At night they drank beer and sang songs. Alex, whose father was swallowed up by one of Canada's deepest caves, or Kyle, whose father was later found split in three at the edge of a retreating glacier, thrummed an acoustic guitar. They wrote poems about their missing fathers and shared them with one another, the rule being that (constructive!) criticism was okay if and only if the author said it was. The fact that all their fathers were frozen here in the same ice fields, the same network of caves, brought a kind of cohesion to the group, the way that being Jewish and in Jerusalem and being rising high school juniors or seniors had once brought a bunch of complete strangers together.

Hence his ambivalence when, in year five, he broke up a block of ice and found inside his father's corpse, eyes wrenched wide open, mouth agape, a coil of rope frozen around one shoulder. He realized at once that the body, which he had last seen when he was, like, six, meant nothing to him, that his father, whom he hardly remembered, meant little to him, and that what he'd actually valued was his father's *absence* and everything connected to it, especially this great group of like-minded guys. His first impulse was to cover up the discovery, pretend it never happened, "keep looking" for his father for the rest of his life along with everyone else, but someone (Kyle?) saw the body and gave a shout and they all gathered around to congratulate him.

Typically, when the son of a vanished ice climber finally finds his father's frozen body, that's that. He takes the body home, buries it, and you never see the guy again. But the next year the son came back to Banff National Park "just to help out." Outwardly everyone was appreciative, but secretly they thought it was a little weird. Like, move on. He even contributed a poem, which some people actually found disrespectful, his father's corpse having been located and the poetry group really being intended for sons who were still searching, and when it came time for "constructive" criticism they did not hold back, calling it indulgent and solipsistic and almost bringing the son to tears.

{ 35 }

PRACTICAL JOKE

....

A mathematician in the field of knot theory was known to be a great practical joker. In fact, he became better known for his practical jokes than for his mathematical program, which was essentially a dead end—a long, failed attempt to prove something called the Kaiserling Conjecture. His son also became a knot theorist, and a very talented one. But he was notoriously solemn, particularly compared to his rambunctious father. He rarely smiled. The father often lamented his son's poor sense of humor.

The old man got lung cancer. On his deathbed, he beckoned for his son, who put his ear to his father's mouth. "The solution to the Kaiserling Conjecture is in my papers," the father whispered. Then he was dead.

The old man's papers were legendarily voluminous, and the son spent the next fifty years poring over them in search of this supposed proof. He never married or had children or even traveled outside the United States. He merely sat amidst his father's papers and read.

At seventy, having read his father's writings down to the last scraps, and finding nothing resembling a proof of the Kaiserling Conjecture, the son finally realized that his whole life had been a practical joke played on him by his father. While the son does not find this funny himself, he reportedly understands why other people might find it funny.

THE TALLINN HOLOCAUST MEMORIAL MUSEUM

....

Three times the opening of the Tallinn Holocaust Museum, a striking postmodern structure intended to evoke the enormity and incomprehensibility of the Holocaust, was delayed after the architect's father (himself a survivor) declared during an advance tour that the museum "was nothing like the Holocaust." In 2003, in 2008, and again in 2011, the architect's father, Zvi Engelmann, flew from Tel Aviv to Tallinn for the ribbon-cutting, said that the museum was "nothing like the Holocaust," and returned to Tel Aviv.

David Engelmann knew, as his wife always reminded him, that he was trying to represent the Holocaust, not reproduce it, but he was evidently distressed by his father's judgment, since each time his father said it was nothing like the Holocaust, Engelmann asked the Estonian government to postpone the opening of the museum. In 2003 he brought in new materials, in 2008 he rethought the proportions, and in 2011 he radically overhauled the sculpture garden. Yet after each change his father declared the museum "nothing like the Holocaust." And between visits he'd sometimes call up his son to say hello, and add, seemingly out of the blue: "Your museum is nothing like the Holocaust." Engelmann began avoiding his father's calls in hopes of, among other things, avoiding the sentence, "Your museum is nothing like the Holocaust," so his father started leaving voicemails, and leaving the sentence there.

The remarkable patience of the Estonian government—remarkable and, as Engelmann would learn later, when he was commissioned to design the headquarters for a leading Estonian investment bank, remarkably *un*Estonian—ran out at last. They would cut the ribbon in 2014, they announced, with or without Engelmann's blessing. His father was by this point in poor health and reluctant to travel. They spoke infrequently. Nothing would have been easier, in other words, than to cut the ribbon without flying in his father. But instead he begged his father to come, and his father did come, and after one glance at the museum he said it was "nothing like the Holocaust." Engelmann took his name off the project, and the following day the museum was unveiled to ecstatic acclaim.

{ 37 }

REPRODUCTION

....

A Newton tutor was paid handsomely by the town's lawyers, consultants, and investment professionals to take their sons and daughters and transform them into younger iterations of themselves, thus ensuring that Newton's money stayed in Newton. One day, however, the tutor found that he could no longer in good conscience help the plutocracy reproduce itself. He gathered up the sons and daughters of the elite of Newton, and also of adjacent Brookline, Wellesley, and Weston, and led them to a self-storage facility in Framingham and locked them in, standing upright, packed tightly together.

The four wealthy suburbs launched a statewide search for their children. After a year they gave up and held a series of somber but well-catered memorial services.

A decade later, the tutor invited the mothers and fathers of the missing children to the Framingham storage facility. With a flourish he flung the rolling metal door upward, expecting the dead sons and daughters to topple over at their parents' feet. But

instead they walked out perfectly healthy, a third of them lawyers, a third of them consultants, and a third of them investment
professionals. They were a little thin and a little thirsty, but basically they were fine, and financially they were doing *extremely*
well. To this day the tutor has no idea how it happened. He was
paid handsomely for finding them.

{ 38 }

FOOTSTEPS

....

A poet and a physicist at the same East Coast college each had a son on the very same day. Each hoped that his son would follow in his footsteps—the poet's son into poetry, the physicist's son into physics. But it was not to be. By the time the boys turned three, the poet noticed that his son had a *physical* view of the world and the physicist noticed that his son had a *poetical* view of the world. One night, while their wives were asleep, they effected a son exchange. The poet and the physicist were exceptionally careful—they cut their sons' hair, exchanged their clothing, and so forth—and the next morning their wives were none the wiser.

The exchange was a terrific success. The physicist's son became a first-rate poet, developing his sham father's poetic style in interesting ways and enhancing both of their reputations. The poet's son, meanwhile, became a superlative physicist, and proposed an ingenious theory that explained many of his sham father's experimental results. The poet and his wife loved their sham son, and the physicist and his wife loved *their* sham son.

It was, in short, an ideal situation.

As it happened, the poet's son and the physicist's son both went on to teach at the same West Coast college, and each had a son on the very same day. The poet's biological son—the physicist—had long, unbeknownst to his parents, been terribly depressed, and he prayed for his own son to do anything *except* physics. The physicist's biological son—the poet—was also, unbeknownst to his parents, terribly depressed, and he prayed for his son to do anything except poetry. Eventually they needed to effect a secret son exchange of their own, after the poet's son noticed that his son was scientifically inclined and the physicist's son noticed that his son was poetically inclined.

Not long after, the poet's son and the physicist's son and their wives all died in a fire, and the grandchildren were sent to live with their grandparents. The poet's son's sham son—a nascent poet—was sent to live with the original physicist, and the physicist's son's sham son—a nascent physicist—was sent to live with the original poet.

So it happens that the elderly poet and his wife are now in fact raising their own grandson, a future physicist, and the elderly physicist and his wife are now raising their own grandson, a future poet. The elderly poet and physicist are rumored to be plotting a secret exchange.

{ 39 }

NEMATODES

. . . .

Two biologists, archenemies, fought for nearly fifty years over the status of two parasitic nematode worms cut out of two beetles collected in the Belgian Congo during the 1930s. Hertzberg contended the worms were of two different species; Berger claimed they were of the same species. Their mutual hatred flared up frequently in the major worm journals and at every important worm forum.

In middle age, Hertzberg came to realize that the debate would outlive both him and his enemy. He swiftly sired three sons, hoping that one of them would be interested in nematode biology, but all three went to astonishing lengths to avoid it—one going so far as to join a company that produced inflatable exercise balls specifically for use in offices.

Hertzberg found himself without followers. For similar reasons, Berger did, too. So when Berger died at age 72, Hertzberg could by all rights have claimed victory: the worms are of *different* species. But instead he toasted Berger and drank a vial of poison he had set aside for just this occasion.

40

VERB INFLECTIONS IN AN ALGONQUIN DIALECT

....

In 1918, the second son of the great German American an-thropologist Franz Boas submitted to his father's *International Journal of American Linguistics* an analysis of the grammar of a language native to the northern reaches of Manitoba, now spoken, he claimed, by just 300 people. An interesting feature of this language, explained Boas's son, is that verbs are inflected not for tense but only for the relative geographic position of the speaker's father—for instance, "I lift (Father is ahead of me to my right) a load out of the canoe," or "The sky snows (Father is behind me to my left.)" The speaker, concluded Boas's son, "lives in a perpetual present, oblivious to and unconcerned with the chronological sequence of events, but highly attuned to the rel-ative location of his father, to his left, to his right, ahead of him, behind him, or diagonal to him."

Worried about his son—whom he knew to be living near

Boston, not northern Manitoba, and engaged in some sort of business enterprise, he was not sure exactly what, but not linguistics—Franz Boas took an early train out of New York and reached his son's apartment by nightfall. It seemed to have been evacuated in a hurry and was more or less empty except for a journal lying open on the floor, the final three entries of which read: "Father is coming," "Father is coming," and "Father is *behind* me to my *right*."

41

CONTROL

. . . .

Two years ago a Serbian sculptor exhibited fifty surreal death scenes of his father at the Baltimore Museum of Art. The sculptor told an interviewer that the surreal death scenes were not intended to take pleasure in the death of his father, who was still alive, but to prepare himself for it, to steel himself for it, to inure himself to the inevitable catastrophe. Sculpting these surreal death scenes gave him the illusion of control over it, he said, the way Freud's grandson had once simulated with playthings the disappearance of his mother. But his father's death last week so closely resembled the nineteenth surreal death scene, including the wheels, the wings, the horns, the hooks, the bed made of moss, the anthropomorphized fruit, and the gargantuan hands, that the sculptor himself has become a suspect.

{ 42 }

SIEGEL'S SHOES

. . . .

Siegel's Shoes, that Chicago landmark, opened its doors in 1869 and threatened to close them again exactly 101 years later, in 1970, when Barry Siegel's two sons, both at that point pursuing physics degrees at the University of Chicago, both expressed extreme reluctance to replace their retiring father and take over their family's shoe store. But Barry insisted, in a manner even more extreme. He broached the conversation again and again. In the end it was Neil, the older of the two, and in fact the more naturally gifted in physics, who acquiesced and took over the shoe store, and Leonard who became the theoretical physicist.

The two brothers, one now filled with guilt and one with resentment, soon stopped speaking to each other, but Siegel's Shoes survived.

Thirty years later, with a fruitful physics career at its apex, having produced two interesting though ultimately untestable ideas about the tiniest of entities, and one interesting untestable idea about an enormous entity, plus a poetic book about the nature of time (cyclical/illusory), the younger Siegel brother, standing at a chalkboard in Oslo, where he had been invited to give an illustrious lecture, suddenly had the distinct, totally disorienting, and, as he later described it, utterly terrifying impression that he was holding not a piece of chalk but a gentleman's foot.

He dropped the chalk, lurched backward. Three Norwegians rushed to his aide.

"I'm fine!" he cried, holding them at bay with his palms. "Really, I'm fine."

He cracked his knuckles and picked up the chalk, accompanied by the horrible sensation that he had merely cracked his knuckles and picked up the foot, and as he brought the chalk to the board to finish writing an equation he perceived with a violent clarity that he was, in reality, slipping the gentleman's foot into an elegant loafer. How, he thought, feeling at his back the compassionate glare of the concerned Scandinavians, do they feel, he thought, letting the chalk slip from his fingertips as he ran from the auditorium.

He did his best to forget the episode. He blamed fatigue or dehydration. But in three later lectures back at the University of Chicago he felt the distinct sensation, three times at the same chalkboard, that he was in actuality slipping three gentlemen's feet into three elegant loafers and asking them to take a little walk around.

Either, thought Leonard, this is a *psychological* breakdown, in which my suppressed guilt over my older brother's life is now making itself felt in an increasingly intrusive fashion, or it's a *physical* breakdown, in which the parallel universe where I became the shoe salesman and he the physicist is flickering into the one where I became the physicist and he the shoe salesman. (Flickering multiverses, as it happens, was one of those untestable ideas on which he'd made his name. They also played an important role in his popular poetical time book.)

The obvious thing to do was to call his older brother and ask him, point-blank, whether he had ever had the sensation, while slipping a gentleman's foot into a loafer, that he was in reality writing an equation on a chalkboard. "Yes" would mean physical breakdown, "no" would mean psychological breakdown. But after some thirty years of basically no relationship it was hard to ask your brother *anything*, much less a question directed at precisely the thing he was most sensitive and aggrieved about, i.e., that he'd spent his entire life handling men's feet rather than fundamental equations, leaving you free, as far as your father was concerned, to work with equations not feet.

So instead of asking, he drove up from campus one day and stealthily pressed his forehead to the chilly windowpane of Siegel's Shoes, with the idea of inferring from the behavior of his brother—who was at that moment crouched attentively in the crotch of a flushed fat man in suspenders, brandishing a brown loafer into which (he seemed now to be explaining the logistics of it to the suspendered fat man) he was proposing to stuff the latter's vast left foot—whether he sometimes flickered, the moment he put a shoe onto a foot, into the parallel universe in which he was a physicist explaining at a chalkboard the fundamental nature of reality.

The fat man proffered his foot. His brother brought the loafer toward it at an angle. Leonard held his breath. His older brother did not appear to be flickering between all conceivable universes. The suspendered fat man's toes breached some invisible plane within the loafer, prompting his brother to expertly reduce the angle in order to glide the gentleman's foot in further, and . . . there.

There!

There it was.

He had expected something subtle, but this was impossible to miss, this combination of physical signs indicating that his brother had instantly flickered into, and back from, an alternative but equally feasible universe in which he stood at a chalkboard, writing a set of equations that together characterized the motion of a certain particle. The customer noticed nothing—he looked down and his enormous foot was elegantly shod—but in that instant his salesman had flickered (at approximately the speed of light) between two of the probabilistically possible universes Barry Siegel had unwittingly brought forth in 1970, and which, Leonard reasoned logically at the windowpane, family members are always unwittingly bringing forth in their interactions with one another. Of course the greatest source of parallel universes, numerically speaking, Leonard reasoned, are fathers who attempt to dictate their sons' careers, thereby instantly bringing forth the universe in which their sons obey their career choice and the universe in which their sons disobey, as well as the infinite array of universes in which their sons are probabilistically smeared between obeying and disobeying; but fathers are not the only world creators; in fact, any interaction between family members brings forth at least one, and usually more than one, universe, especially an interaction that carries with it a demand; and a corollary he could deduce from this before even removing his forehead from the windowpane was that bigger families, as well as more inter-active families, bring forth more universes, and big interactive families who make lots of demands on one another bring forth the most universes, numerically. (He was not saying anything about the quality of these universes.) In terms of the physics it was not necessarily wrong to call any conversation with a loved one a universe-splitting juncture or nodal point, and one's will-ingness to enter into such a conversation should depend solely on one's willingness to be smeared probabilistically between all possible outcomes.

Leonard wrote up the paper in a single sitting, working out in a sort of frenzy, but with the utmost mathematical rigor, the worlds Barry Siegel had brought into being in 1970 with his al-most inhuman shoe store obstinacy. There was the world in which Leonard did fundamental physics and Neil sold men's shoes, the world in which Neil did fundamental physics and Leonard sold men's shoes, the world in which both did physics, the world in which both sold shoes, and the infinite array of worlds in which Leonard and Neil were each probabilistically smeared between doing theoretical physics and selling men's shoes.

Observing, by the paper's own logic, that in half of these feasible universes it was Neil and not Leonard who authored it, Leonard put down his brother as his coauthor and sent it to him at Siegel's Shoes for his perusal. Amazingly, his older brother's pride (Neil responded in a terse little note that he had "never once envied you or regretted my decision to take over Dad's store," and demanded that his name be removed from "your unbelievably condescending article") blinded him—*whether or not he agreed with Leonard's mathematical analysis of it*—to the undeniable phenomenological fact that the Siegel brothers were perpetually flickering back and forth in their professional lives, both at times scientists, both at times proprietors of Siegel's Shoes, which stands to this day in each and every one of these possible worlds at the corner of Monroe Street and State, and is now the oldest continuously operating shoe store in Chicago.

{ 43 }

BREATHING PROBLEMS

....

A son who moved back into his childhood home as an adult
has become unhinged by his father's audible breathing, which is
impeding the son's literary-philosophical writings. The father's
nose or sinuses must have changed over the years, according to
the son, who in childhood never heard air rustling into or out of
his father's nose. He has persuaded his father to see an otolaryngologist.

The mother's breathing is also audible, so she, too, will see an
otolaryngologist.

These otolaryngology visits should hopefully shed light on
what is happening to his parents' nasal cavities.

{ 44 }

THE CONVERSATIONALIST

....

Ever since an evidently pivotal LSD experience in western Norway in 1971, the great Icelandic artist Karl Karlsson—until then an undistinguished landscape painter—has painted nothing but colossal canvases of two heads in conversation. Critics generally interpret the series as a long-running inquiry into the very possibility of conversation.

Although Karlsson's earliest heads (1971–1976) seem to be involved in a genuine exchange, subsequent decades (1976–1997) saw a continual diminution in the size of their mouths. By 1998, Karlsson's abstract interlocutors were entirely mouthless, and they remained so until 2009.

This is typically considered the most pessimistic phase of Karlsson's career.

Since then, the mouths of his heads have been growing once more. Karlsson's critics, collectors, and advocates cheered: it seemed that he had found new faith in the possibility of authentic human interaction. But there were signs by early 2012 that the mouths on his heads were getting a little *too* big, and by 2013 the mouths were clearly *much too big* for the heads. The mouths now take up most of the heads, and there are indications that one of the two heads—the one on the left—will actually swallow the other head, the one on the right, whole, probably as early as 2019.

It is interesting to note that Karlsson is not, as one might assume, some sort of recluse. He lives half of the year in London and is said to be exceedingly social, and a superb conversationalist.

45

THE STIPULATION

....

A famous performer, celebrated around the globe for his singing and dancing, added to the detailed rider for his most recent tour the stipulation that his father must be kept "a certain distance" from him at all times, a distance "not greater than three hundred feet and not less than thirty feet." According to the tour rider, the performer was unable to perform if he was too close to or too far from his father, a retired postal worker. When he was too close to his father he could not dance, and when he was too far he could not sing, the rider explained. Between thirty and three hundred feet was the proper range.

This did *not* mean, said the rider, which the performer is rumored to have written himself, that the father should be kept a fixed distance away from him at all times, such as 165 feet. Optimally, in the hours preceding a concert, the retired postal worker should be brought closer and then taken farther away, brought closer and then taken farther away, brought closer and then taken farther away, though of course *never brought closer than 30 feet or taken farther away than 300.* The periodic near-ness and remoteness of his father was the only way to ensure that the performer could perform to the best of his ability, according to the rider: "The oscillation of the father is critical to the success of the engagement."

Someone from the performer's management company leaked the tour rider to the Internet, and the performer was, pre-dictably, ridiculed for his demands. But I've noticed that most of the ridicule has come from women. Men—at least in the com-ment threads I have seen—have been largely sympathetic, many noting their own shattering realization as adults that they could exist neither near nor far from their fathers and would spend the rest of their lives moving cyclically toward and away from them in an endless attempt to determine the *ideal distance*—which was probably, they knew, a chimerical concept. If they could in-struct venue employees to ferry their fathers toward and away from them in a continuous oscillatory fashion, never coming too close or going too far, they absolutely would.

46

RESEMBLANCE

....

For nearly his entire career, the son of the great Dutch architect Willem de Waal has had to explain (ad nauseam) that while his buildings do bear a superficial resemblance to his famous father's buildings, they're in fact "a foot shorter" and "feel completely different." A careful and honest comparison of his new Arrivals Terminal at Schiphol to his father's legendary Terminal 2 at Chicago O'Hare—two structures which a critic at *De Telegraaf* libelously called "identical"—would show that the son's building is one foot shorter and just *feels* completely different. His Gateway Arch of Guangzhou, which has drawn comparisons to his father's Gateway Arch of St. Louis, is actually one foot shorter than that arch, and *feels* completely different. His neofuturism and his heavy use of catenary curves obviously owe something to his father's neofuturism and use of catenary curves, but in the son's aesthetic they feel completely different, and are one foot shorter.

Yesterday, at the unveiling of his design for the Brussels

Museum of Modern Art, which will be a foot shorter but otherwise identical to his father's San Francisco Museum of Modern Art, de Waal launched into an attack on the architectural establishment, which he accused of becoming "fixated" on elements like form, color, style, light, scale, texture, material, and so forth, to the utter neglect of "feel" and "height difference."

47

CORRESPONDENCE

....

The son of Salzburg's most profound modern philosopher and the son of New York's most brilliant modern composer, each of whom is said to be totally inept when it comes to understanding his father's work, have refused all calls to publish the voluminous correspondence that their fathers exchanged over the course of a forty-year friendship, correspondence that scholars believe would shed a great deal of light on their intricate, elusive theories and symphonies. The philosopher's son is worried his father comes across as *mean*, and the composer's son is worried his comes across as *gay*.

{ 48 }

A BAD MODIGLIANI

....

You think you're learning something from someone; you always realize too late that you're just turning into him. When you learn a little bit from someone, you've turned into him a little bit, and when you learn a lot from someone you've turned into him completely. So it was for a young artist who learned to paint by studying Modigliani, and realized deep into his study that he was only learning to paint *like Modigliani.* He vowed never to gaze upon another of Modigliani's sensuous, languid, elongated faces or figures, at the risk of falling permanently under his sway.

Had he, perhaps, caught himself just in time? It was true that his own faces and figures were not especially languid or elongated, and after his first exhibition not a single critic—all of whom, incidentally, believed they'd *learned* from earlier critics when really they had just *turned into* those earlier critics— mentioned Modigliani as a possible influence.

Soon his career was thriving. Dealers, who believed they had learned from earlier dealers, not just turned into them, courted him, and collectors, who believed they had learned from earlier collectors, bid up his work. Not once was Modigliani ever alluded to in connection with his art. He was sui generis, a modern master. And, of course, he began to believe this himself. He became sanguine about the possibility of education, gave money to art schools, stressed the importance of studying past masters, and neglected to mention that when you exhaustively study an Old Master, the Old Master studies you, the first- or second-year art school student, equally exhaustively. He omitted his earlier suspicion that art museums are little more than big buildings where rectangular old men, hung on the walls by their backs, wait for young people to come stand in front of them.

But amid all this success, something began happening to his face, and something began happening to his figure. His face was becoming more and more languid. As for his figure, the only word for it, by the time he turned forty-five, was "elongated." Altogether he was rapidly becoming increasingly sensuous.

The painter tried frantically to hide these transformations. On his face he wore at all times an alert, dynamic expression that was intended to undercut his increasingly languid features. He never allowed the least note of dreaminess to enter his eyes, and he was vigilant lest his fingertips drift indolently along his jawbone. To mask his elongated figure he wore shirts with horizontal stripes, and around his obscenely stretched neck he experimented, for the first time in his life, with scarves.

But no matter what he did, it was obvious to all that he was becoming ever more languid, ever more elongated, and ever more sensuous. "What wistful sensuousness!" others marveled, in whispers, without yet connecting him to Modigliani. Once he nearly lay nude, on a blue cushion, very much like the woman in Modigliani's *Nude on a Blue Cushion*, before catching himself, and sitting instead fully clothed, on the couch.

He looked so familiar, everyone said! Who did he look like? They couldn't place it. He lived the rest of his life in mortal fear of someone finally making the Modigliani connection. But no one did. When he died, of alcoholism, he was the most revered artist of his day. Only at his funeral did it dawn on everyone that he looked, languid in his coffin, like a bad Modigliani. As soon as he was put in the ground, his reputation began to decline.

49

FIND AND REPLACE

....

The author of a book of anecdotes or jokes about his father—not this book—got a phone call from him just minutes before he planned to send the book to an agent. The phone call was so pleasant, so unusually effortless and intimate, that the author had second thoughts about his whole project, on which he'd spent years. When he hung up the phone, he burst into tears. He had told his father everything about the project, all of the formal challenges he had faced in the writing of it, all of the hopes he had for it—everything except the fact that it was about *him*.

The book strove for "honesty," whatever that might mean, yet now he felt more duplicitous than ever.

So, at the last minute, the author pressed Shift-Command-H to open the Find and Replace window in Microsoft Word and replaced every "father" with a "mother," every "dad" with a "mom." He figured his truths about fathers were basically transferable to mothers—who also, after all, come before us and create us and mold our thoughts and who are also disappointed and confused by us when we distance ourselves from them in order to work out which of our thoughts are *our* thoughts and which of our thoughts are *their* thoughts, a project which, if we're completely honest with ourselves, we never make any headway on and which isn't even *our* project to begin with because we learned it from our literary and philosophical mothers and fathers (and so, instead of liberating ourselves, we're just choosing our literary-philosophical parents over our birth parents).

Yes, he told himself, this is about *parents*. Everything he'd written about fathers applied to mothers, too. We try (and fail) to wrest our heads from our mom's hands just as we try (and fail) to wrest them from our dad's hands.

He sent the document to the agent. "A book about my mother," he wrote.

But the fundamental noninterconvertibility of mothers and fathers was brought home to him moments later when the agent asked if he intended to refer three times on the first page to his "mother's penis."

50

THE FAMILY *RIVULIDAE*

....

In 1863, the Swiss ichthyologist Rudolf Fehrmann, whose theory linking the complexity of freshwater fish to the existence of God had been ridiculed in Darwin's *On the Origin of Species*, watched his son, Conrad, set off from the port of Hamburg on a sailing vessel called the *Rondelet*. Conrad was to restore honor to the Fehrmann name by sailing to Uruguay and catching from the rivers there a tiny freshwater fish of the family *Rivulidae*, a fish so ingeniously designed, particularly in its reproductive system, according to his father, that it would, his father said, at once vindicate his theory and deal a humiliating death blow to Darwin's. "Go," his father exhorted him on the dock, not without tenderness. "Bring me that tiny Uruguayan fish."

But Conrad was a Darwinian. He had never admitted this to his father, of course, and as he watched the archaic ichthyologist shrink on the dock, waving his arms happily overhead, Conrad felt an indescribable pang. For instead of sailing to Uruguay and fulfilling his father's mission, he sailed to the nearby town of Wilhelmshaven, where he dismantled his ship, dispersed his crew, and exchanged the name Fehrmann for Pflug.

He never saw his father again.

He did, however, keep up with one or two ichthyology journals, and from those pages he gleaned that his father never lost hope that his son would return with the Uruguayan river fish that would destroy Darwin. Forty years later, when his father was 101 and evolution a settled issue among ichthyologists, Rudolf wrote to the *Journal of Fish Biology* that his son ("a brilliant scientist in his own right") would "soon sail into Hamburg harbor with a tiny Uruguayan fish of the family *Rivulidae* that will create massive problems for Mr. Darwin." He died a few months later, and Conrad eulogized him in the same journal. "If anything indicates the inadequacy of natural law," Conrad wrote, "it isn't the intricate gonads of a Uruguayan river fish but the uncanny faith of a Swiss ichthyologist."

51

THE UPPSALA SCHOOL
OF METEOROLOGY

....

The example of Fehrmann's son was cited repeatedly in 1938 by the Swedish meteorologist Gustaf Almqvist, father of the Uppsala School of Meteorology, whose son Gunnar disappeared in early January of that year after flying straight into the center of an enormous extratropical cyclone in order to disprove his father's so-called Uppsala Model of Extratropical Cyclone Intensification.

The elder Almqvist, weirdly unperturbed by his son's missing plane, explained to the journalists who gathered outside his office that Gunnar had subscribed to the Uppsala orthodoxy on the genesis and decay of extratropical cyclones, but not on their intensification. On the birth of cyclones he was "an Uppsala man" and on the death of cyclones he was "an Uppsala man through and through," said the elder Almqvist, but on the intensification of cyclones he was "profoundly anti-Uppsala." On the beginnings and endings of extratropical cyclones you could not wish for a more faithful Uppsala apostle, but on the intensification issue it was hard to find anyone more un-Uppsalian, so much so that in some ways he was actually closer to the Gothenburg School.

The fundamental question was whether air temperatures in the core of an extratropical cyclone were *very cold* (Gustaf) or *moderately cold* (Gunnar) compared to the surrounding air. Three months prior, Gustaf had once again reiterated his belief that the core air was "very cold," Gunnar had replied that the air was only "moderately cold," Gustaf had called him "a Gothenburg man through and through," and not a word had passed between them since.

Only now did the elder Almqvist, cocking his head slightly, show a little emotion: "I ought to have said 'You're a Gothenburg man *on the intensification question*, otherwise Uppsala.'"

It soon emerged that the peculiar equanimity of the elder Almqvist in the face of his son's disappearance stemmed from his absolute conviction that Gunnar had flown into the core of the cyclone, sampled air that was *very* (not moderately) cold, and resolved to vanish, airplane and all, much as Fehrmann *fils* had almost a century earlier, albeit for different reasons, rather than return to his father with his wounded pride and his refuted cyclonic beliefs. When a reporter for the *Svenska Dagbladet* suggested he at least consider the possibility that both airplane and son really had been lost in the storm, which was in fact of historic intensity, the elder Almqvist merely laughed. "He sampled some very cold air and vanished, that's all!" he said.

The next day, bits of the young Almqvist's plane were found floating in the North Sea. These bits—none of which, after all, were wings, propellers, or other components of special aerodynamical consequence—did not seem to trouble his father greatly. "Just come home," he said, addressing his son in an interview with *Dagens Nyheter*. "Bring the air temperature measurements." The next night the plane itself was found incinerated in a field near the town of Hanstholm in northern Denmark. The elder Almqvist told reporters that his proud son must have ejected himself upon noting the coldness of the core air and was now living in Denmark or perhaps by this point Germany, along with his evidence of a *very* (not moderately) cold cyclone core. But the Swedish newspapers felt now that they would be exploiting an obviously distraught and delusional old man to print these thoughts, or his pleading with his son to "come home, with or without the measurements, though preferably with," so the journalists wrapped up their articles and left Uppsala.

That, plus political events, pushed the cyclone tragedy off the front page. But Almqvist, who suffered a stroke in '42 and was bedridden thereafter, asked his extensive network of students to keep an eye out for a tall Swedish meteorologist with a fake name who held down-the-line Uppsala positions on the genesis and decay of extratropical cyclones yet was trying to hold onto a Gothenburg-like model on their intensification, *in the face of his own empirical air temperature data.* For a long time he heard nothing, but in 1947, shortly before his death, he received an anonymous letter, which may have been a prank, informing him of the appointment of a new M.I.T. professor who seemed to match that exact description.

THE KONIGSBERG BUILDING

····················

The billionaire banker Konigsberg made major donations to three top business schools—Harvard, Stanford, and Wharton—so that his son, who was only seven at the time, would have his "pick of the litter." By the time the son applied to business schools fifteen years later, there were Konigsberg Buildings and Konigsberg Gardens on all three campuses. He decided to go to the school with the tallest Konigsberg Building, which was Wharton, and after the first day of class he flung himself off the top of it. He landed, however, on the soft mulch of the Konigsberg Garden, thus surviving the fall and losing only the use of his legs. Since then, thanks to another substantial donation from Konigsberg's father, Wharton has worked hard to improve the accessibility of its facilities for people with disabilities. Today, Wharton boasts the most accessible business school campus in the world.

{ 53 }

TALENT

....

Details have emerged regarding the recent case of patricide in our town. It seems that the perpetrator had been living rent-free in his father's attic for ten years. According to court transcripts, the son was attempting during that decade to write a single short story, which was itself about a father and son. For five years the father let the son write, but in the sixth year he began pestering him to see some pages. One member of the jury told the press that the father simply wanted some evidence his son "actually had talent." Finally, in year ten, the father issued an ultimatum: if the son wouldn't show him his short story, he would evict him from the attic.

The son hatched a plan to humiliate his father. He knew very well that his father had *already made* his judgment—that his son had no talent—and would therefore deem anything he showed him a failure. He also knew that his father knew nothing about literature. So the son typed up a canonical short story—Kafka's "The Judgment"—and presented it under his own name. When his father inevitably dismissed it, according to court transcripts, the son would reveal that he had "just dismissed Kafka" and was thus no authority on literary matters.

That evening, after reading, his father came up to the attic, which he hadn't done in years. The son was shocked to see tears in his father's eyes. "You have a great talent," his father supposedly whispered, pulling his son into a rare embrace. "I'm sorry to have doubted you."

According to court transcripts, the son was so bewildered by his father's reaction that he simply said, "You have just dismissed Kafka," and struck him on the head with a large wrench. The father died hours later in a local hospital.

Probably as a result of the trial publicity, a national magazine actually agreed to publish the murderer's short story next week. I'm eager to see it. It is reportedly hugely derivative, but not of Kafka.

{ 54 }

EXPLOITATION

....

A leading American photographer of the latter half of the twentieth century, whose artistic career had been financed by his father's once-famous but now-shuttered Fifth Avenue department store, Kern's, achieved his greatest success with a series of frank, ruthless photographs chronicling his father's senescence, including that legendarily wrenching shot of the frugal old man scrubbing, without the slightest show of emotion, his soiled undergarments in his bathroom sink. In a brief artist's statement the photographer said simply that the work was an attempt to "understand my father and my relation to him."

Thirty years later, the photographer, now roughly the age his father had been in those photographs, declared that he intended to buy back from galleries, collectors, and museums each and every one of them. He spent the rest of the still-considerable Kern's fortune in doing so. Then he piled the photographs in a barn on his Berkshires farm and set the barn on fire.

The media descended. Every newspaper in the world tried to

interview him. He turned down all of them but his local weekly, the *Lenox Ledger*. Here the photographer explained his realization that under the guise of trying to "understand" his father, he had merely exploited him. Throughout his career, he told the interviewer, whenever he said that he wanted to understand something (*through* his art), he really meant that he wanted to exploit it (*for* his art). There was nothing to understand about his father, there was only something about him to exploit. There was certainly nothing to understand about death, the other ostensible subject matter of the photographs, only something to artistically exploit. And so forth. Everyone, he said, but in particular artists, humanists, journalists, social scientists, and natural scientists, ought to banish the word "understand" from their vocabularies and replace it in every instance with the word "exploit."

The photographer died of a brain tumor the following week.

The world consists of nothing but cheap ironies: really, only the cheapest. So no sooner had the eminent photographer excoriated the concept of "understanding" and died of his tumor than the world—especially the art world, the media world, and the academic world—erupted in attempts to understand him and his motives for destroying his greatest works of art. (No one, needless to say, took him at his word.) A couple of neuroscientists emerged to explain, more or less, that the photographer's tumor had impinged on the portion of the brain normally responsible for preventing people from burning down their own art-filled barns. A woman with, inexplicably, a TV show conjured up out of almost nothing several decades of child abuse, both of the photographer by his father and by the photographer of his own son. But the most convincing explanation—convincing, I admit, even to me, despite my sympathy for the photographer's rant— came from one jaundiced critic writing online at the *New Yorker*. Drawing attention to the man's declining reputation in recent decades, including the almost total neglect of his career retrospective the previous year at MoMA, the critic suggested that the destruction of his greatest photos was actually the photographer's final exploitation of his father—one last, desperate bid for immortality, which he'd come to realize would not issue from the photos themselves. By burning the photographs of his father, he was trying to ensure his permanent notoriety. The critic proposed seeing the photographer's career as three successive exploitations of his father and his father's department store: first as funding, then as subject matter, then, finally, as "combustible material for his eternal flame," which, the critic predicted rather coldly, would actually "burn out within ten or fifteen years."

{ 55 }

PEACE PLAN

....

The insane son of the Israeli prime minister and the insane son of the chairman of the Palestine Liberation Organization, patients at the same Jerusalem psychiatric hospital, have accomplished what their supposedly "sane" fathers have never been able to: they have agreed on a peace plan for the Middle East. Although the peace plan makes little sense and seems not to refer to the world in which we live, the simple act of these two men, one Jewish and one Muslim, both profoundly psychotic, meeting in the TV room every single day and shaking hands for up to twenty-five minutes at a time while chanting, in unison, at the top of their lungs, the demented terms of their "peace plan"—this simple act may, we hope, serve as an inspiration to their fathers.

THE INVERTED PYRAMID

....

In January, the Stupendous Bosches, a family of acrobats celebrated for their "inverted pyramid" trick, collapsed while per-
forming the inverted pyramid at a circus in Bremen. Six Bosches
across three generations were killed.

Only the bottom Bosch, the tip of the inverted pyramid, survived.

This happened on the very same day, at the same hour, that
Professor Pasternak, the distinguished mathematician whose
family had long ago formulated the Pasternak Problem in combinatorics, leaped to his death from the top of St. Isaac's Cathe-
dral in St. Petersburg.

Professor Pasternak was survived by his son, a fellow mathematician.

There was, of course, no reason to suspect a link between
these two tragedies. But when Bremen police spoke to the bottom Bosch, and Petersburg police spoke to Professor Pasternak's
son, they made an unlikely discovery: the bottom Bosch was a

Pasternak, and the last Pasternak was a Bosch. Police in both cities were stumped, and neither Bosch nor Pasternak would say another word.

Berlin's best detectives were sent to Bremen. *How had a Russian mathematician infiltrated their nation's most beloved upside-down acrobatic configuration?* Moscow dispatched its best detectives to Petersburg. *How had a German acrobat infiltrated their nation's most esteemed mathematics department?*

Eventually it emerged that Bosch, the youngest son of the Bosch acrobatic clan, and Pasternak, the youngest son of the Pasternak mathematical dynasty, had met by chance on a riverboat cruise of the River Daugava in Riga, where one (Bosch) had come to perform with his family's circus act, and the other (Pasternak) had come to speak on his family's problem at a combinatorics conference.

According to a Latvian computer programmer who was also on the cruise, the two men were initially amused by their physical resemblance, which was striking, Bosch's beard notwithstanding. They started talking, comparing their respective responsibilities as the most recent offshoots of two legendary families.

The conversation grew heated. Evidently, each believed his burden was the more onerous.

In the inverted pyramid formation Bosch had to physically support three generations of male Bosches on his shoulders. His father stood on his right shoulder, his brother on his left shoulder. On his father's shoulders stood his paternal grandfather and his great-uncle, and on his brother's shoulders stood his maternal grandfather and a first cousin twice removed. All this a hundred feet in the air, on a high wire. One wobble and his entire family fell to their doom, shouted Bosch. And they weren't just standing there, they were juggling, a stream of machetes flying back and forth between the grandfathers, not to mention the great-uncle's five flaming torches, et cetera!

Pasternak merely laughed, the Latvian programmer recalled.

So Bosch had six living Bosches standing once a night on his back, is that right? asked Pasternak. That's nothing. He had *twelve generations* of Pasternaks, both living *and* dead, standing *at all times* on the surface of his *brain,* in a treacherous variant of the inverted pyramid you might call a *vertical column formation.* Twelve generations ago, in 1744, his ancestor presented the Pasternak Problem to the Imperial Russian Academy of Sciences. He spent the rest of his life thinking about the problem, but he failed to solve it. So did the next ten generations. So did Pasternak's father. And now it fell to him. He had been given every resource, every advantage. His father had even cut short his own mathematical career to provide his son with a top-notch mathematical upbringing. All the best schools, the best teachers. Training in Germany, France, and America. He had nearly three hundred years of past Pasternak thinking to draw on. It was, as his father put it almost every morning, time to solve this thing.

That, said Pasternak, is what I call a burden. Twelve dead men standing in a column on my brain. I would kill to have six live family members juggling on my back! I would feel as light as a feather!

My God, said Bosch the acrobat, what I would give to feel nothing but the purely symbolic weight of your dead ancestors.

It's heavy, said Pasternak.

I bet it's not actually so heavy, said Bosch. What's heavy is six physical jugglers.

The deal was struck then and there, the Latvian programmer told authorities. Pasternak would grow a beard and pretend to be Bosch; Bosch would shave his beard and pretend to be Pasternak. The first to capitulate to the pressure of the other's family had to buy a round of beer.

Bosch taught Pasternak—who luckily spoke fluent German from his studies—the rudiments of acrobatics, and Pasternak taught Bosch—who spoke fluent Russian from his travels—the rudiments of combinatorics. Then Pasternak went with the circus to Bremen, and Bosch went with Professor Pasternak back to Petersburg.

Disaster struck both families immediately. In Bremen, six Bosches climbed onto Pasternak's back, his knee wobbled, and they all fell to their deaths. In St. Petersburg, Bosch bungled a simple mathematical operation and Professor Pasternak realized that his son would never solve the Pasternak Problem. He went straight to St. Isaac's and flung himself from its golden dome.

Presented with the evidence, Pasternak and Bosch confessed.

The Germans wanted Pasternak to pay, and the Russians wanted Bosch to suffer, but the best lawyers in both countries could not find a German or Russian law that they'd actually violated. Reluctantly, the police released them. They met up three days later in a Riga bar, where they split the cost of the round of beer. Freed from their acrobatic and mathematical obligations, each planned, exuberantly, to spend the rest of his life pursuing his actual passion: birding for Bosch and backgammon for Pasternak. But at that moment, Riga police burst in and hauled them off. It seems Latvia has an old, seldom-enforced law on its books forbidding the sale or barter of one's dynastic duties. The penalty is death.

{ 57 }

FIGMENTS

....

A solipsist at New York University who'd convinced himself through ironclad argument that the world was a figment of his imagination submitted as his philosophy dissertation two selections from Hume's *Treatise of Human Nature* and four from Wittgenstein's *On Certainty.* Of all of the figments of his imagination, the student explained to his committee, he was proudest of the figment Hume and the figment Wittgenstein, whom he had considered his two principal influences before he realized they were actually his own creations.

The student was surprised when his dissertation committee—composed of two tenured figments of his imagination and one younger, untenured figment—accused him of plagiarism. He was brought before the University Disciplinary Board but declined to defend himself. It would be the height of insanity, he said, to defend himself before a University Disciplinary Board *of his own creation.*

He now lives at home with his parents in Demarest, New Jersey, a suburb and state of his own creation. His mother, a museum docent, acknowledges that she may well be a figment of his imagination. His father, a rather obstinate real estate attorney, maintains his metaphysical independence.

THE CONSTITUTIONAL LAW
SCHOLAR'S TRAITS

....

A renowned constitutional law scholar combined in one person intellectual verve, ethical decency, and physical elegance, but his three sons, to whom he'd hoped to pass on these three admirable traits, each inherited only one of them: the oldest son inherited the verve, the second son the decency, and the third the elegance.

In time, these traits, so valuable in combination, destroyed their lives.

Everyone who recognized the father's familiar intellectual verve in the oldest son also expected, naturally, the concomitant decency and elegance. When it became evident that these traits were absent, his verve became a sign of what he lacked, and although the son was not especially immoral or inelegant in absolute terms, he nevertheless developed a reputation as a *grotesque reprobate*. Similarly, the second son's ethical decency wasn't admired on its own terms, so to speak: it merely marked the absence of his father's verve and elegance, and though the son was not especially intellectually lethargic or physically inelegant compared to the population at large, he nevertheless became known as a *mentally disabled monster*. The third son, who had his father's elegance but no particular verve or exceptional decency, was called a *handsome depraved moron*. These reputations followed them, needless to say, through their lives and to their graves.

An interesting coda. Each of the three sons had a son of his own, identical to him in every respect. The first son's son inherited the verve, the second son's son the decency, the third son's son the elegance. By this time, though, the constitutional law scholar had faded into obscurity, so the presence of each trait no longer signified the absence of any others. Thus the grotesque reprobate's son was simply considered *brilliant*, the mentally disabled monster's son *righteous*, and the handsome depraved moron's son *suave*.

{ 59 }

SALVAGEABLE

....

From his father he had inherited a heart with an arrhythmia condition, a mind with a melancholy disposition, a house with an insulation problem, and a tree with a fungal infection.

His cardiologist friends assured him, however, that his arrhythmia was treatable, his yogic buddies maintained that his melancholy was ameliorable, his contractor pals claimed that his home was weatherizable, and his arborist chums swore that his tree was salvageable.

Everything can be fixed, they insisted. Everything can be made like new!

But very politely he has declined all their help. No thank you to the cardiologists, no thank you to the yogis, no thank you to the contractors, and no thank you to the arborists (one of whom even specializes specifically in decay-causing fungi). What point, they wonder, is he trying to make, exactly, by sitting in that cold house with that irregular heartbeat and that sad head, beside the diseased tree?

{ 60 }

MASTERS

. . . .

A son who rebelled against his father, repudiated his father's belief system, left his father's home, and became after some time
the disciple of another master, was distressed to discover that his
father and his master had met each other, liked each other, got
coffee together now at least once a week, and often went on little
weekend outings around New England together.

He felt betrayed, of course, but also perplexed. He had se-
lected this master precisely for the ways in which he was different from his father, almost his opposite. If they ever met, he'd
once thought, they wouldn't understand each other at all. The
same words would mean something radically different to each of
them. So how to explain all these classic New England outings?
Three weekends ago: Newport, Rhode Island. This past weekend:
the Berkshires. Clearly, they *were* able to communicate. Either
his father and his master were not as different as he'd thought,
or they'd forged a simple common language, a sort of pidgin

tongue, that made these classic outings not only possible but actually pleasant, even delightful.

The moment he discovered his father's Tanglewood ticket stub in his master's recycling bin, the son knew the apprenticeship was finished. He renounced his master, repudiated his master's belief system, and left his master's home. At length he found a third master, one diametrically opposed to the other two. His philosophy was different, his concepts were different, his very vocabulary was different! There was, it seemed to the son, no common ground between them. Yet no sooner had he entered this master's tutelage than the master met and hit it off with his father and his second master and all three went on a classic New England getaway, to tour the covered bridges of Vermont. The following weekend, they drove to the peak of Mt. Washington. The weekend after that, a quintessential New England outing to Martha's Vineyard.

The son repudiated the third master and entered the tutelage of a fourth master, who only days later was enjoying lobster rolls with the other three in Portsmouth, New Hampshire.

The son repudiated the fourth master and entered a period of self-reflection. He had sought a master *nothing* like his father, to furnish him with a philosophy *unlike* his father's. Yet each successive master must actually have been *very much* like his father, and very much like the others, for how else to account for the fervor with which they explored New England together? Men with incommensurable and irreconcilable worldviews do not pile into a car together every weekend, or every other weekend, and drive for up to four or five hours to see the best of what New

England has to offer, now lighthouses along the coast of Maine, now foliage in the Connecticut River Valley. Either, the son reflected, all masters were, by nature, men like his father, with the same values and the same pedagogies and the same notion of what a perfect New England weekend looks like—or else the only men who *appeared to him* to be masters were men like his father. In other words, maybe he was seeking out, without even realizing it, men of his father's temperament, with his father's philosophy, and his father's eagerness to really get to know his pretty little corner of the country, with its interesting colonial heritage, and calling them "master." Maybe that, to him, was just what a "master" was.

Either way, the son realized, he was on his own from now on. There was no point in becoming the disciple of another man who would only end up as another buccaneer of this little New England sightseeing brigade, which that very weekend was off picking its own pumpkins and gourds from a supposedly glorious pumpkin patch near Brattleboro, Vermont.

SOMETHING TO GENETICS

. . . .

The son of the infamous Chessboard Killer, who killed his victims by pushing them into open manholes and tallied them by placing one pebble per victim on a chessboard in his apartment, vowed to save lives rather than take them. For this reason he became a nurse, the very converse of his father. However, as one pundit put it, "there must be *something* to genetics," because at some point last year the son started murdering huge numbers of people himself, also by pushing them into open manholes. Just like his father, he kept a tally of his victims by placing individual pebbles on the squares of a chessboard.

{ 62 }

ASSISTED LIVING

....

The so-called Surrogate Sons Program at a Cleveland assisted-living facility has been altered to better suit the needs of its residents. In response to complaints that the frequency, willingness, duration, and mood of the surrogate sons' visits were all undermining their authenticity, facility administrators have asked the surrogates to visit less frequently, less willingly, for shorter stretches at a time, and with more unspoken resentment and visible unease. During a meeting this fall, a number of surrogates shared tips on how to make the experience as realistic as possible. Mr. Solomon's surrogate son likes to begin a game of Rummy 500 but leave well before either player reaches 500 points, with an excuse that cannot help but indicate the bustling, populated nature of his life. When Mr. Nolan's surrogate comes to visit, it's like he's only interested in using the pool and sauna. "I wait until Mr. Nolan's telling me about the moment in the 1950s when he realized communism was misguided, and then

I suddenly ask how late the sauna's open," the surrogate shared. Mr. Wellerstein's surrogate sends him an email every so often saying he might not be able to visit until March; when March rolls around, the surrogate simply doesn't show up (or even send an email explaining why). Next time he emails, he just pretends like he never said anything about March. Soon he starts emailing about a potential visit the *following* March. On his comment card, Mr. Wellerstein rated his surrogate son experience a five ("Excellent") and noted, in the space for additional comments, that he was "looking forward to March."

But perhaps the most instructive case is that of Mr. Shapiro. Mr. Shapiro has not yet heard from his surrogate son, a silence that reminds Mr. Shapiro, he told administrators, of his actual son's silence. Lately, when Mr. Shapiro, a survivor of the Leningrad blockade, cries out, terrified, in the night, he calls not for his *son* but for his *surrogate son*. The nonarrival of the surrogate son faithfully mimics the nonarrival of the actual son, neither of whom, according to Mr. Shapiro, can be blamed for leading a full life and being busy with career and family. His actual son once suggested recording an oral history of his father's experiences during the Leningrad blockade, but he has not followed through on the idea and probably never will. The surrogate son has also, realistically, never recorded an oral history of Mr. Shapiro's blockade experiences. The nonrecording of the surrogate is indistinguishable from the nonrecording of the actual. Mr. Shapiro rated his surrogate son experience a five. "What a splendid service!" he effused. It was only when administrators looked up his surrogate son, with the idea of having him speak at their fall meeting, that they realized Mr. Shapiro had not signed up for the Surrogate Sons Program and had never been assigned a surrogate. Still, they consider his case a model of what the program can, at least in theory, hope to achieve.

{ 63 }

VENGEANCE

· ·

They were in line at the deli when a black-haired man crept up to his father and shot him twice at close range, for reasons the boy was too young to grasp. He was seven years old. *One day,* he thought, as the black-haired man slipped into the crowd, *I will find you and I will kill you.* But as the years went by, and he became familiar with the ways of the world and the complexity of all things, and the chains of causation that tie each act to the future and to the past, he came to realize that he could probably get away with not doing it. Plus, how would he even find him?

A NIGHTMARE

....

A man had a nightmare that his dad had a heart attack and died.

When he woke up, he vowed to eliminate the chilliness that had insidiously invaded their relationship.

He tried to call his dad, but continually pressed the wrong numbers on his phone. He knew the right numbers, he could see them, but he could not press them with his fingers. Later he saw his dad across the street. He tried to run to him but could not move his legs.

Now the man realized he had simply awoken from a nightmare *within* a nightmare. He was still, so to speak, in the outer nightmare.

In the next scene, he met his father for dinner. They tried to hug each other, but could not. Again the operations of dream logic. They *knew* how to hug, there was no real obstacle to a hug, there could be nothing easier than to hug. But here they were, standing essentially side by side, interlocking just one arm apiece, thumping each other energetically on the back.

Somehow he managed to order food and begin eating. He tried to speak, but—no surprise—could not. His father spoke, but in a very strange language. No, it was English, the son realized, but he still couldn't understand what his father was saying. Then he did begin to understand it, but he could not understand why his father seemed to care so *much* about whatever it was he was speaking about. Then the son's own mouth fell open and he spoke about some things *he* cared about, and his father didn't seem to understand why he cared about them at all. Subsequently, they alternated between the father speaking about the things *he* cared about and the son speaking about the things *he* cared about. Neither, in accordance with the dictates of dream logic, could admit that what the other one was saying meant absolutely nothing to him.

After dinner he and his dad "hugged" again.

None of this upset the man too much. He knew he was dreaming. Even after ten years—in dreamtime—had gone by, he knew he was dreaming. One day he got a phone call informing him that his father had had a heart attack, and he woke up.

He realized that his father had been dead for twenty years.

Then he woke up again, this time to what was indisputably the outermost stratum of reality. His relationship with his father had actually never been better. But the fact that he was capable of such dreams even when things seemed to be going *well* concerned and saddened him.

{ 65 }

VANISHED

. . . .

In the early Edo period, two samurai, a father and son, were disgraced when their lord's army was routed in battle. The son asked permission from his father to commit suicide, but the father said, "Wait a minute. It's not right that a son should die before his father." He handed his sword to his son, who cut off his father's head and prepared to thrust the sword into his own stomach. But he found, to his amazement, that the desire to kill himself had suddenly vanished. Now he wanted to go into the mountains and compose haiku about the changing seasons (especially the change from summer to autumn). His three servants, however, were regarding him with an air of expectation. "It is not right," the son said, "that a master should die before his servants." So the three servants thrust their swords into their stomachs and the samurai went into the mountains and spent the rest of his life writing thousands of haiku about the change from one season to another, several of which, particularly the melancholy death-conscious summer-to-autumn ones, all fallen leaves and so forth, are seen today as masterpieces of the form.

66

THE FAMILY SHIRAZ

. . . .

A Barossa Valley winemaker, whose prized Shiraz was consistently awarded 98 points by the influential wine critic Robert Parker, was laid low last year with a herniated disc, at which point he reluctantly relinquished control of the vineyard to his son. For over a decade the winemaker had been promising that the vineyard would pass one day to his son, but only now, with the herniation of his disc, did he finally follow through on that pledge.

His reluctance was justified: his son instantly instituted changes at every stage of the winemaking process, from growing to bottling. The famed family Shiraz was altered beyond recognition. The son assured his father that the changes were for the better: they were "innovations." The father, on the other hand, who had been making Shiraz his way for thirty years, was certain that his son was making unnecessary changes simply to "make his mark," to demonstrate his autonomy. And the wine, he believed, would suffer for it.

But they awaited the final judgment of Robert Parker's newsletter. A 99 or 100 would vindicate the son. A 97 or below would vindicate the father. And another 98 would reveal to them the ridiculous, almost ceremonial aspect of their intergenerational conflict, a ritual that had little to do (or so a 98 Robert Parker score would indicate) with the actual quality of the wine.

The newsletter arrived. They opened it nervously, but were perplexed to find in it no numbers at all. A note explained that control of the newsletter had passed from Robert Parker to his son, David, who had replaced his father's outmoded numerical rating system with an updated star-based system. "There is no basis of comparison," he wrote, "between my dad's numerical rating system and my star-based system. Our systems are fundamentally incommensurable. There is no common measure. They cannot be converted, they cannot be translated. They do not communicate. Each constitutes its own self-contained, self-consistent, sealed-off world of wine opinion."

The prized Barossa Valley Shiraz was awarded *seven stars* by David Parker. How that compares to a Robert Parker score of 98 is unknown. The father and son have no one else to appeal to in order to adjudicate their dispute.

67

ABUSE

. . . .

The estate of an author who died thirty years ago has sued the young author of a book whose style and theme are so derivative of the dead man's that the latter must be considered, they claim, the true author of it, despite being dead.

The young author, whose father happens to be an eminent intellectual property lawyer, has countersued on interesting grounds. He concedes that his book's style and theme are those of the dead author, but denies stealing them. Rather, he claims that the author's style is so potent and his theme so forcefully expressed that they were, in fact, imposed onto him against his will. The year during which he read every word the dead author had ever written (which at the time seemed like the most liberating year of his life, and which led to his quitting law school and taking up fiction) was really, in retrospect, a period of extreme emotional, psychological, and intellectual abuse. The countersuit also accuses the dead author of what it refers to as "conceptual and categorical abuse," or abuse in which the abuser's concepts and categories are inflicted on the abused, who comes to view them as intrinsic to the nature of things and can no longer think about reality in any other terms. The defendant's father—who has had a personal animus toward the dead author ever since his son quit law school, for which he was uniquely well suited—even introduced an insinuation of sexual impropriety, claiming that the dead author "forcibly inserted his conceptual scheme" into the then twenty-four-year-old's head.

On the fourth day of the trial, the young author took the stand. No one could deny that when he opened his mouth the dead author's thoughts fell out, expressed in the dead author's unmistakable tone and syntax, premised on his concepts and categories. But was this a case of conceptual *theft* or conceptual *abuse*? Had a vigorous young man stolen the work of a vulnerable dead author, as the estate maintained, or had a vigorous dead author pressed himself upon a vulnerable young man, as his father contended?

The case ultimately hinged on whether there was some pith, some essence of the young man underneath all that extrinsic thought and foreign insight. If yes, then the pith, the essence, could be held responsible for plagiarism. If no, if the dead author's thinking went all the way down, so to speak, if there was no *person* there to do the impersonating, then the young man, who did not exist, could hardly be considered anything but a victim. So the lawyer was put in the uncomfortable position of arguing that his son, his erstwhile pride and joy, was now nothing more than a vehicle for the dead author's thoughts, while the estate had to argue that the young man existed in a more substantive fashion than his own father gave him credit for. The young man monitored all this with the dead author's wry detachment and the dead author's death-haunted fatalism.

The jury is expected to deliver a verdict later today.

LEGACY

. . . .

For most of his life, Nathan was referred to as "the son of the famous atonal composer." Even after three well-regarded jazz albums of his own, *none* of them atonal, Nathan was still referred to as the "the son of the famous atonal composer." No matter what I accomplish in my life, Nathan told friends, I will *always* be referred to as "the son of the famous atonal composer." Today, however, he is almost universally referred to as "that jazz trumpeter who took out his penis on an airplane."

CRUSHED

....

A medical student, the son of a famous obesity scientist and himself a budding obesity scientist, began a relationship about three years ago with an obese paralegal. This huge paralegal had no redeeming qualities, according to the medical student's friends. When asked why he was dating her, he would simply say that he liked the sensation of being *crushed* by the colossal paralegal.

Everyone suspected the medical student of somehow rebelling against his father, the legendary obesity scientist, the very first to call obesity an epidemic, but the medical student assured everyone that, no, he just enjoyed the sensation of being physically crushed by this genuinely enormous and not especially friendly paralegal.

Finally he proposed to her. His father at first refused to attend the wedding, but at the last second he had a change of heart and sped to the synagogue. Halfway there he was struck by a garbage truck and killed. On hearing the news, the medical student, breathing what to more than one guest seemed like a sigh of relief, stopped the wedding. His friends and family assumed he would break off the engagement and settle down with a woman of normal dimensions. But as of now the medical student is still engaged to the paralegal, and she is apparently bigger than ever.

70

THE OTTOMAN HISTORIAN'S HEAD

....

Nearing the end of his long life, the Ottoman historian began hinting to his two sons, in ways subtle and not so subtle, that he wished to be cryogenically frozen upon his death, and resurrected whenever the needed technology became available. By the very end the historian managed to steer *every single conversation* toward his own cryogenic freezing and subsequent resurrection. His sons were taken aback. For years he had spoken about the fullness and richness of his life, the importance of dying gracefully, and so on. But now the Ottoman historian's eyes glimmered with fear and he often cried, apropos of nothing, "Freeze me!"

I doubt any two sons have ever agreed on the question of their father's cryogenic freezing. These two were no exception. The older brother was vaguely pro-freezing, the younger brother stridently anti-freezing. He, the younger, stressed the exorbitant cost of the procedure, the great absurdity and indignity of it, the unlikelihood that it would even succeed. He implied that their father—who during this very conversation sat on a couch in the other room yelling, "Put me in a special freezer!"—was not in his right mind. The older brother countered that neither of them could grasp the unfathomable terror of imminent nonexistence. The eleventh-hour urge to be frozen was probably completely rational, he said, something that would one day seize them, as well.

At an impasse, they brought in their father and asked him point-blank *why* he wanted to be frozen. The old man was quiet for a moment and then said that he had not finished thinking about the Ottoman Empire.

Neither of the sons, needless to say, was happy with this answer, and they decided to bury their father rather than freeze him. Still, to comfort him in his remaining days, they got an estimate for how much it would cost to keep his head frozen for ten thousand years, and even forged and signed a fake contract to this effect. At the same time, they secretly paid cash for a burial plot, which was obviously cheaper, though surprisingly not *that* much cheaper. I hear the Ottoman historian's last words were: See you soon!

71

THE LABOR
HISTORIAN'S HEAD

....

That is not the only cryogenic preservation story I know involving a historian and his son, oddly enough. What is it about historians, their sons, and the promises and possibilities of cryogenics? In any case, this other, rather more personal story, which involves a historian not of the Ottomans but of American labor movements, has a happier ending, sort of.

This historian's son, whom I met during my horrible year in Los Angeles, offered me a beer once in exchange for notes on his screenplay. I accepted, not for the beer but in hopes of making a friend. He sat me on his I think rotting sofa, brought me a glass of Diet Coke—turns out he didn't even have any beer—and a copy of his script, and shut himself in his bedroom. (He said he didn't want to "overhear" my reactions.)

The script was bad. I read slowly, painstakingly seeking out details to praise while formulating at the same time a "general reaction" that I immediately realized would have to be completely mendacious, and after ten pages I took a break under the pretense of getting more ice for my soda. I strolled into the kitchen and came upon two large freezers sitting side by side. Some heavy-duty leather work gloves hung from a hook attached by magnet to one of them. All in all, a strange setup.

I called out, "Which freezer for ice cubes?"

"Left one," he called back.

"What's in the right one?" I asked, but then answered my own question by lifting the lid and finding inside the frozen head of a middle-aged man. His eyes were open. He looked a little judgmental. His prominent nose was thickly encased in ice.

"My father's frozen head," said my friend, coming into the kitchen. "Don't tell me how the script is!" he added quickly, raising both palms toward me. "Just don't say anything until you've read the whole thing. I know it's bad."

"No," I lied. "Not at all."

"It's terrible, I know. But I want it all at once. Your critique, I mean. Also, even though he's dead and frozen, I don't like talking about my scripts in front of my father."

He put on the leather work gloves and picked up his father's frozen head. That was the sole purpose of these gloves, it seemed, picking up this ice-encrusted head.

"Probably curious why I have my dad's frozen head in a freezer," he said.

"Not if you don't want to talk about it."

"I don't mind. Want to hold him? There's another pair of gloves under the sink."

"No, thank you."

"It's nothing, it's just like holding a big icy rock."

"Is it safe out of the freezer? It won't, like, melt?"

He addressed the head as one would a baby: "Oh, we won't let you melt, will we, Daddy?" Then, to me, he added, "He can be out for approximately fifteen minutes. Have a seat. Ice cubes are over there, by the way. So, what do you know about cryogenic freezing?"

I told him I actually knew of an Ottoman historian who was *nearly* cryogenically frozen, and in fact *believed* he was going to be cryogenically frozen, but unbeknownst to him was buried instead.

"Interesting. My dad was a historian, too."

"Of what?"

"Of American labor movements." He held up his father's frozen head in front of his own and intoned humorously: "*In that year the AFL and CIO merged to become the AFL-CIO.*"

"Ha."

"*Samuel Gompers,*" he intoned humorously, behind his father's head. "*SAMUEL GOMPERS.*"

I laughed again, but I was thinking: I really hope I would treat my father's frozen head with more respect than this guy treats his father's frozen head.

The funerary circumstances of the labor historian were, it emerged, rather different from those of the Ottoman historian. The labor historian wanted to be cremated, not preserved at very low temperatures. "*I* was the one who wanted him frozen," the son admitted.

On the table a small pool of water was forming under his father's frozen head. I said, "Shall we put him back in the freezer? This is making me a little nervous."

"I've done this like a million times," he said, sort of annoyed, as he sponged up his father's water with a rag and tossed his script, which I'd brought into the kitchen, to the far side of the table, out of range of the runoff from his father's head.

The father wanted to be cremated, the son wanted him frozen. Why? Because, when the father died a decade ago, the son was at a "low point." He had dropped out of college. He was making *collage art*—the ironic inflection is his—in Berlin. He had been operating under the assumption that he would have at least twenty or thirty more years in which to achieve success and impress his father, a respected public intellectual with a prestigious chair at Princeton. But instead his father died abruptly of pancreatic cancer at fifty-two. "You died thinking I was a failure," my friend said tragically to his father's frozen head, whose fleshy left ear was now almost entirely thawed out.

Was he killing his frozen father right in front of me? Killing, I should say, any hopes of future reanimation? He kept sponging up more and more of his father's head water with that sopping rag and wringing it out one-handedly over the sink. What else could I say, though? "Put your father's decapitated head back in the freezer, or I'm outta here"? That would sound rather dramatic. If the guy wants to let his dad's head thaw out, I thought, let him thaw it out. It's none of my business.

Now his father's eyebrow ice was melting. One silvery strand poked free at a ferociously intelligent angle. As the layer of ice over his eyes thinned, I noticed that he seemed less judgmental and more just sort of skeptical and disappointed.

"Look at that!" my friend cried, pointing at his father's eyes.

"What?"

"See the pupils kind of darting back and forth a little bit?"

"Are they?"

"He's trying to read my screenplay from all the way across the table." My friend shut the script and admonished the head: "No! No!"

"The neuroscience of it is pretty fascinating," he whispered to me. "There are still brain waves. Not enough to have a conversation or anything, but he's constantly trying to read my screenplays. Can I ask you one thing about what you've read so far, by the way?"

"Sure."

"Never mind," he said, shaking his head. "I'll wait till you finish. It's about the scene at the laundromat, which you probably already got to, but I'll let you finish first."

Thank God. The laundromat scene was *awful*.

He returned to his story. Only once had he suggested the idea of cryopreservation to his father, right before he died. His father had ridiculed the idea. "The last bauble rich folks can buy," he'd said, and then repeated his wish to be cremated. Those were his last words.

Ordinarily his mother would have taken the lead on the funeral arrangements, but she was too distraught, my friend said. So she gave her son enough money for a decent cremation and trusted him to take care of it. Bad idea. He took the money and his father's corpse to a budget cryogenics facility. Bad idea number two. The budget facility was all he could afford with the cremation money. At first they seemed competent enough. They cut off the labor historian's head and stored it in a fancy-looking freezer. So far, so good. But three years later the company was bankrupt. They announced that the freezers would be unplugged at the end of the week. What could my friend do? He ran to the cryogenics facility with a bag of ice from 7-Eleven, took his dad's frozen head home, and stuck it in the freezer. Later he bought another freezer, wholly devoted to the head. "Hence the dual freezer arrangement," he said with pride, perching his father's head on his lap and thumping both freezers at once.

The last seven or so years of his life, his father's frozen head had accompanied him everywhere. He went back to college, and his father's head came, too. The frozen head looked relieved during that period, according to my friend, who even remembers seeing a faint smile. Then they moved to Manhattan, my friend and the head, for a job interning at Scott Rudin's film production company. That was a hard year. Every night when he got back to his Alphabet City walk-up, there was his dad's head in the freezer, looking a little dubious. A kind of *is-this-what-you-really-want-out-of-life?* expression, according to my friend. Then things got worse. Rudin fired him. The head was furious! From its face it was clear the head wanted to have a little chat with Mr. Rudin. The son was tempted. He actually put his father's head in a bag of ice, hailed a cab, and was halfway to Rudin's office before he realized what a huge mistake he was making. If he hoped to succeed in the biz, he probably didn't want a reputation as "that guy who brought in his father's frozen head to confront Scott Rudin." He had the cab turn around. That night he stayed up till three talking to the frozen head, and the next morning he applied to film school at USC.

They drove out to L.A. together. "That was an *amazing* road trip," said my friend wistfully, resting his chin on his father's half-thawed head. Some of his dad's head slush smeared off onto his chin, which was weirdly touching. "We were probably closer during that trip than we'd ever been before," he said.

But film school was a bust. He could tell from his father's head's expression that it was a lot less rigorous than the head had expected. It was no history doctorate, that's for sure. His father's expression, he said, went from dubious to disappointed. "Look!" he said, pointing at his father's face. "Even right now, as I'm telling this story, he's thinking I should have gotten a Ph.D. in history. The man is obsessed! In case you were wondering," he said to the thawing head, "this is *precisely* why I don't take you out of the freezer so much anymore."

He covered his father's big, unfrozen ears with his hands. "I quit film school," he confided. "He doesn't know that yet. Right now I'm just one hundred percent focused on writing this screenplay, and for money I work at a Coffee Bean."

He uncovered his father's ears and said loudly, "So, when I get my film degree, we'll see what happens."

"It's been fifteen minutes, by the way," I said.

"You can stand another five," said my friend to the head. "Can't you? You don't want to be cooped up in that freezer again, I don't think."

Just then a whole sheet of ice calved off the frozen head's heavily-lined forehead and hit the floor, liquefying on impact. "Fuuuck," my friend groaned. He pointed at a cupboard. "Mind snagging the paper towels?" As I kneeled down to mop up the forehead puddle, I noticed—I don't think I was inventing this— that the father's head was trying to catch my eye. He was almost thawed out. All that remained was a thin coating of ice over his slightly parted lips. He looked a little panicked.

"So," I asked with forced nonchalance, "what happens when he's fully melted?"

"I've only gone this far once before," said my friend. "Last time, when his mouth ice melted, he murmured something to me. I'm curious if he'll do it again."

"After that you should really put him back in the freezer."

"Yep, after that, back he goes."

As the father's face grew more and more agitated, and we waited for the melting of his mouth ice, I inquired about the current state of reanimation technology. How long from now till they're able to resurrect the man?

Again he covered his father's ears.

"They could do it today," he said. "The technology's there. *I'm* the holdup now. I'm waiting until I, you know, achieve something. I don't want him back until he can be proud of me. Is that ridiculously selfish?"

"No, not at all."

"It is, isn't it? That's why so much depends on this screenplay. I know it's got some structural problems, but I'm kind of hoping it's the one."

"I hope so, too," I said, knowing it was not.

The last piece of ice slid from his father's open mouth and hit the floor. The son, solemn all of a sudden, lifted his father's now totally unfrozen head and put its mouth to his ear like a conch shell.

Sure enough, the lips moved.

There was a raspy, rabbinical sound.

Then the head said something.

I missed it, but evidently the son did not. He put his father's head back on the kitchen table, snatched his script, stomped into his room, and slammed the door.

The labor historian's head stared at me, terrified.

Hastily I found the other pair of head-handling gloves under the sink and returned the head to its freezer. The head seemed relieved, but also very sad and very alone.

As I slipped out of the apartment I could hear the son ripping up page after page.

• • •

But I said there was a happy ending, sort of.

A little while later my friend gave me a call. "Really sorry for how things ended the other day," he said. "That must have been kind of awkward for you."

"No, no. Not to worry. How do things stand with your father's head?"

"Well, not so good."

"No reconciliation?"

"Not as such. Listen. You guys seemed to get along pretty well. I noticed how he kept catching your eye."

"I think he was just scared."

"He liked you, obviously. And that's fine. Actually, that's great. I was hoping you could take him for a while. I can't really write with him in the freezer. I'm happy to struggle, but I can't struggle with my father's frozen head in the other room, do you know what I mean?"

"Absolutely."

"It's just hard to do the whole struggling-Hollywood thing with your father's head twenty feet away in a freezer, if that makes any sense."

"It makes perfect sense."

I pictured life with the labor historian's head, and I liked what I saw. I have kind of a distant relationship with my own father, who is extremely supportive but a bit aloof, so I felt that I might really benefit from a judgmental visage in the freezer.

I said, "I would be very happy to take him off your hands for a while."

"Thanks," he said. "Thank you. Seriously."

"No problem."

"I owe you one."

"It's my pleasure."

"Promise me one thing, though. You can't resurrect him until I've made it."

I knew by that point that he would never "make it" in Hollywood, or probably anywhere else, but still I said: "I won't, I promise."

My friend—it occurs to me now that that's the wrong designation—brought over his father's head in the big freezer, and I never saw or heard from him again. But the labor historian's head and I embarked on a pretty wonderful little life together. We saw a lot of the world. He improved my life in a number of ways, personally and professionally. And a few years later, while the son was still flailing around L.A., I broke my promise and had his father resurrected. They affixed his head to an animatronic body and zapped the whole thing with an ultraprecise amount of electricity. So, he's back now. He's back at Princeton, too, where he teaches a popular lecture course called *Work in America*. Just one semester a year, a sort of semiretirement. He's a great guy. Our relationship is a little more complicated—obviously—than when he was a just a frozen head, but it's still very, very solid. We talk about everything. The only thing we never talk about is his son.

IMPROVEMENT

· ·

A particular line of male lab rats has exhibited, from generation to generation, a marked improvement in maze performance, suggesting that the skill may in fact be heritable. The first rat in this line completed the maze in one minute and fifty-nine seconds. His sons finished the maze in an average time of one minute and forty-two seconds. The third generation ran it in an average time of one minute and twenty-five seconds, and the fourth generation finished it on average in one minute and seven seconds. Unfortunately, the trend ended with the fifth generation. After an hour in the maze, the fifth generation of rats had still not budged from the starting line. It is not known whether they were *unable* to move or *unwilling*. They were also unable or unwilling to mate, so the experiment has since been discontinued. Upon dissection, their brains were found to be pathologically large.

{ 73 }

PRINTING ERROR

....

By twenty-nine, he had funneled some of his father's billions into the movie industry. Yet instead of being called a "human money funnel" or a "prominent human tube," or even a "major fiscal shunt," he's described in a recent issue of *Forbes* magazine as "one of the most successful young producers in Hollywood."

{ 74 }

THE END OF EVANS

·····················

The humiliating end of Elliot Evans, for many years England's most famous medium, was witnessed by nearly the entire nation.

Evans, who came from a line of psychologists, had made his name in the 1940s and '50s by "channeling" the voices of British soldiers killed during the Second World War. In 1959, the BBC announced that Evans would channel, live on television, Prince George, the only member of the British royal family to die during the war. It is reported that forty million people tuned in to watch the séance. Evans, dashing in his tuxedo, sat onstage with George's son, Prince Edward. Evans took Edward's hand and fell into one of his famous trances. Then—disaster. As all of England watched, Evans began shouting into the Prince's face: WHAT *IS* A MEDIUM? WHAT DOES A MEDIUM *DO*? DO YOU KNOW ANY *OTHER* MEDIUMS? YOU'VE NEVER MENTIONED BECOMING A MEDIUM *BEFORE*.

After a full minute of this, Evans woke from his trance and clambered offstage. The next day he apologized to the nation, explaining that he had accidentally channeled his own father instead of Prince Edward's.

Alas, his ability to channel men other than his father steadily declined, and by the early 1970s he could channel *only* his father, who kept wondering—through the medium of Evans—what a medium *was*, what a medium *did*, whether he knew any *other* mediums, and why he had never mentioned becoming a medium *before*. Evans continued to make a living, but only as a kind of novelty act, and in fall 1981 he disappeared during a long walk in the Scottish Highlands.

75

UTTERLY INSCRUTABLE

· ·

The son of the serial killer who terrorized the greater Tucson area for fifteen years, from 1989 to 2004, granted a single interview after his father's arrest, in which he answered, rather eloquently, the question the country was asking: How was it possible to live under a man's roof for so long and not realize that he's a serial killer?

"I think," he replied, "the people closest to us are sometimes the most opaque to us. Perhaps the closer we are, the more ignorant we are."

Early in the trial it emerged that the son had once discovered four human femurs in his father's sock drawer. He granted another interview. "Even the people we love are, in the end, utterly inscrutable to us," he said. "We believe we have unhindered access to their minds, but we actually have no access whatsoever."

Later it came out that the son had once found two human heads simmering in two large cauldrons on the stove. "Even the consciousness that seems nearest to us is still infinitely far away," he explained in an interview.

The family ate human hearts and owned a quilt stitched from skin, at home the father wore a necklace made of toes, and on another occasion the son discovered three human heads simmering in three cauldrons on the stove. "Another person's mind is always a mystery to us," the son said in his most recent interview.

76

THE MADMAN'S TIME MACHINE

....

On the coldest night of the year a madman was taken to Boston Medical Center with third-degree frostbite. Police had found him under an overpass naked in a cardboard box. Scrawled on the box in black magic marker were the words: TIME MACHINE.

Oddly, the frostbitten madman was jubilant.

Until recently, he told the psychiatrist assigned to him, he had been the most intelligent person in history, smarter even than Einstein ("if only by a little bit") and Newton ("if only by a little bit"). But his historic intelligence had been a curse.

"Being able to perceive the true nature of everything instantly is actually awful," he told the psychiatrist. He had grown bored and lonely. The moment he embarked on a thought, he reached its logical terminus. "At some point," he said, "there is just nothing left to think. Meanwhile everyone else is back there at the first principles, the assumptions, the postulates."

He investigated the great problems of cosmology but solved them immediately. In May he ended metaphysics. He turned to the nature of time, which he hoped would divert his mind for at least a few weeks, but the nature of time revealed itself to him in an afternoon. Once again he was bored and lonely. So he built the time machine.

"That right there?" asked the psychiatrist, gesturing at the cardboard box, which the madman had refused to relinquish.

"*That*," said the madman with a strange smile, "is merely a cardboard box."

The real time machine, he said, was obviously much more complicated, and was obviously made entirely or almost entirely out of metal. For a while it had relieved his boredom. He visited the recent past, then the near future, then the distant past, and then the remote future. He sought out the company of his fellow geniuses. He discussed gravity with Galileo and buoyancy with Archimedes. He brought Fermat to the near future and ate future bagels, which are "much puffier and much more moist," according to the madman, than the bagels of today. He met one of the most important thinkers of the remote future, a mammoth reptilian creature with an unpronounceable name, and took him back in time to meet Louis XIV, the so-called Sun King. This meeting, said the madman, was "incredibly awkward."

Soon the madman had talked to everyone worth talking to, seen everything worth seeing, thought about everything worth thinking about, and yet again was left bored and lonely. Even the company of geniuses wasn't enough; boredom would always be with him, he realized, as long as he had this huge, historic intelligence. Suicide was the only way out. He decided to commit suicide by paradox. He would go back in time and kill his own grandfather—a logical impossibility, as we all know, he said, since killing his grandfather would mean he himself wouldn't be born, which would mean he couldn't go back in time to kill his grandfather. So this might be interesting, he said. Plus, he said, he would get to murder the man who'd handed down to him this huge, horrible, historic intelligence.

The madman set his time machine for 1932 Berlin, where his grandfather was a promising Expressionist painter. He materialized in his grandfather's studio with a gun. "*Nein!*" his grandfather yelled, raising his paintbrush, the madman told the psychiatrist. "*Nein!*" He aimed his pistol. His grandmother ran in. "*Nein!*" she said, according to the madman. "*Nein! Nein!*" He fired into his grandfather's chest and the promising Expressionist painter fell over dead.

But the madman didn't disappear. Nor, he said, did the universe implode.

Was there no paradox after all?

As his sobbing grandmother ran over to his dead grandfather, the madman noticed the slight swell of her belly. Ah! he realized, as he recalled to the psychiatrist. She was already pregnant!

That instant the madman vanished from the studio and materialized naked under an overpass in the cardboard box labeled TIME MACHINE. The real time machine was gone. For a moment he was confused. Then everything became terrifically clear. His father had still been born, but now fatherlessly, and his life had gone, instead of well, poorly; instead of becoming a mathematician, he'd become an underemployed roofer. His son, the madman, had no longer grown up in an intellectual milieu. Instead of becoming brilliant beyond bounds, said the madman with evident relief, he had become stupid, and even a little bit insane. And obviously in this alternate universe he was totally and utterly incapable of building an actual functioning time machine.

"Look at it now!" the madman cried joyfully. "A cardboard box!"

77

FLEISCHMAN'S PREDICAMENT

....

Fleischman, the film critic's son, once explained his predicament to me.

His great-grandfather rebelled against his great-great-grandfather over the issue of Judaism; his grandfather rebelled against his great-grandfather over the issue of Marxism; and his father rebelled against his grandfather by becoming a film critic.

The family business, Fleischman realized, is rebellion! He was even expected by his father, the film critic, to rebel! Thus, he realized, as he put it to me over lunch at the Pakistani restaurant in our neighborhood, the only way he could *actually* rebel would be *not to rebel at all*.

By rebelling he would not be rebelling, but by not rebelling he would be rebelling. The Fleischman predicament, he declared.

This was why he was making himself over in his father's image. If I was wondering why he was wearing one of his father's old suits and his father's old glasses, with the prescription lenses popped out and plain glass put in, Fleischman told me at the Pakistani place, *this* was why. *This* was why he was writing unpaid film reviews for our town's free alternative news-weekly. And had I noticed, he wanted to know, that he had even adopted many of his father's speech patterns? "These words are his words!" cried Fleischman excitedly. "It is even possible that these thoughts are his thoughts!" He had also, he said, perfected his father's laugh. He showed me this laugh at some length. By becoming his father, he was, ironically, becoming his own man, Fleischman explained, laughing his father's laugh.

Needless to say, I turned down all future lunch invitations from Fleischman. His father called a few months later to inform me that Fleischman was being hospitalized. I got an enthusiastic voicemail from Fleischman the same night, calling from the asylum. He said that his father's failure to recognize his actions as nothing more than a form of rebellion was a sign that he was rebelling—or rather *not* rebelling—properly. I need to keep doing exactly what I'm doing, Fleischman said, and then hung up.

78

THE BALKAN HISTORIAN

·······················

A soft-spoken Balkan historian at our college was inordinately sensitive to the subtle means by which power operates. For reasons that were never completely clear, he was absurdly careful not to influence us intellectually—consciously or subconsciously—in any way, and always strove in his lectures to separate his Balkan *facts* from his Balkan *interpretations*. At first we assumed this was just his pedagogical philosophy, but later, when it became so clearly pathological, we suspected that it might be connected to his upbringing. (His father was, depending on whom you asked, a Serbian war criminal, a Macedonian statesman, a Croatian optician, or a Bosnian cobbler.)

In any case, the Balkan historian finally broke down during the third of his three lectures on the Congress of Berlin when he realized that he could not give us a single fact about the Congress of Berlin without also impressing upon us, implicitly or explicitly, his judgment or interpretation of it, even if the judgment was simply that it was a fact worth knowing. In the end, he was reduced to stating again and again the dates during which the Congress took place—*June 13 to July 13, 1878*—while inserting intermittently that it was "entirely up to [us]" whether or not we considered these dates to be of any importance.

He resigned his appointment that day and later drowned himself in a local lake. According to a note, he was horrified by the number of students he had unintentionally influenced and imprinted himself on over the years. How could he bear the guilt of *his* Balkan history thoughts occupying *their* heads? (We were confused: we had signed up for the course as much for his thoughts as for his facts.) Only by drowning himself, he wrote, could he prevent himself from ever insidiously influencing another student. Unfortunately, the lake in which he drowned himself was also, unbeknownst to him, a reservoir, and soon the entire college population was virulently ill.

79

GRIEF

....

Visitors to the San Antonio Zoo have long been moved by the sad sight of Samson, an elderly African elephant who spends some fourteen hours a day pushing a huge tractor tire in a circle around his enclosure, moaning the entire time.

Rumor spread that Samson was in mourning for his son, transferred many years ago to another zoo.

His zookeepers, who knew that Samson had never had children and was simply driven insane by the conditions of his existence, thus had a decision to make. They could explain to the public that Samson moaned and pushed his tractor tire in a circle because he was deranged, or they could let the public continue thinking that he did so because he was deranged *by grief*.

Needless to say, they went with the second option. They even nailed a sign beside Samson's pen describing the exceptionally close-knit nature of the elephant family unit.

This seeming confirmation of Samson's circumstance has

attracted more visitors to his enclosure than ever before. They crowd around him. He moans and pushes his huge tractor tire. "A father driven to grief by the loss of his son," they think, never suspecting that he's just a berserk bachelor totally unhinged by every single aspect of his life.

80

TWO MUSEUMS

· ·

The two sons of Portugal's greatest poet agreed, at last, to turn his house into a museum, but they could not agree on its design. The older son, fiercely loyal to his father, wanted to showcase the poet's study, with its simple but sturdy desk, as well as the grand, extensive library and the little garden in which he strolled after work. The younger son, loyal above all, he said, to the *truth*, maintained that the two bathrooms, the downstairs bathroom but especially the upstairs bathroom, had to be the focal point of any "honest" museum about their father. A Nunes museum that did not emphasize the bathrooms, the younger son insisted, was not an "honest" Nunes Museum at all.

The two sons ultimately agreed to split the house and open their own museums: the Nunes House and the Nunes Estate. Both offer guided tours depicting a day in the life of Nunes. The Nunes House tour starts in the bedroom, heads first to the study, then to the library, and concludes in the garden. The tour guide recites poems related to each location. The Nunes Estate tour begins, likewise, in the bedroom, but proceeds first to the upstairs bathroom, then to the kitchen, and then to the downstairs bathroom. The tour guide recites a poem related to this location. The tour guide then sort of wanders aimlessly through the house, shouting at everyone to shut up, he's trying to think, before winding up back at the upstairs bathroom. He recites a poem related to this location. Visitors are then encouraged to journey back and forth between the two bathrooms on their own, following the well-demarcated "Path of Nunes" from the upstairs bathroom to the downstairs bathroom to the upstairs bathroom to the downstairs bathroom, and finally back to the bedroom. Interactive stations along the path invite younger visitors to stop, listen closely, and report, via the touchscreen, whether there are any sounds that might "interfere with your ability to think."

Both museums expect to expand over the coming year, the Nunes House incorporating the meditation alcove in the attic, the Nunes Estate adding the basement half-bathroom supposedly frequented by Nunes during the 1984–85 composition of *The Lisbon Cycle*.

Neither museum, according to Nunes scholars, contributes anything to our understanding of his poetry.

ORDER MATTERS

· ·

His great-great-grandfather was a Belarusian shoemaker. His great-grandfather was a music teacher. His grandfather was a respected attorney. His father reached the very pinnacle of the medical profession, and just days ago was named director of the National Institutes of Health. He himself, like his great-grandfather, was a music teacher. But it is one thing to teach music when your father is a Belarusian shoemaker, and quite another to do so when your father runs the NIH. *Order*, as he put it in his suicide note, *matters*.

DETERMINISM

....

He did not know who his father was, but he could narrow it down to four men his mother had dated in the mid-1980s: a powerful politician, a wealthy industrialist, a wise rabbi, or a sort of artist-slash-tinkerer who had designed an unusual cylindrical fish tank and ultimately hanged himself from a beam in his garage.

As a child, he prayed that one of them (not the despondent fish tank maker) would appear one day and proclaim himself to be his father. That never happened. Upon graduating from college, he was still, as it were, in the dark.

Since his father would not reveal himself, and his mother, if she knew, would not tell him, it was up to him, he realized, to deduce who it was. His only evidence would be himself. Years from now he would take a look at his life. Had he amassed power? Then, he would conclude, he was the politician's son. Had he amassed a fortune? The industrialist's son. Had he amassed wisdom? The rabbi's son. Had he gone into fish tank design? Fish tank guy's son.

He felt a bit like the planchette on a Ouija board, gliding to and fro under ghostly influences. Whenever he felt the urge to command men, to impose his will on society, to punish the wicked and aid the weak—then he felt the hand of the politician. But that urge would be displaced by another: to multiply his resources, to live in luxury, to provide for his loved ones. Those days he was the industrialist's son. But the next morning he would feel empty and unfulfilled. He would seek meaning, simplicity, calm. That was the rabbi in him. But before long he'd have an innovative idea for a fish tank. He would sketch shapes or forlornly diagram new self-cleaning mechanisms. Then he felt the presence of the disconsolate fish tank guy. And that, he was perturbed to discover, was the influence he felt more and more often.

Time went by.

Twenty years later he took stock of things. He surveyed his life. He had no power. He had no money. He had no wisdom. But he had patents pending on two fish tank designs (one with a so-called Algae Eradicating Vacuum Nozzle, the other with his Skim System Automatic Protein Skimmer) and was clinically depressed.

He took the evidence of his life (his tank designs, his depression) and threw them at his mother's feet, demanding that she admit, at long last, that he was the son of the despondent fish tank maker, just as he'd always feared. But she would not admit it. In tears she now insisted, rather belatedly, that he was the son of the industrialist, the "most happy-go-lucky guy," she said, that she had ever met.

How then, he asked, to explain *this* (Protein Skimmer) and *this* (depressed head)?

Desperate, presumably, for him to avoid the fish tank maker's fate, she attributed what was so obviously his genetic destiny to some sort of perverse self-fulfilling prophecy. And that was her line for the rest of his life, a short life of modest fish tank innovation and metastasizing melancholia. Whenever he complained that his life had been completely determined at the moment of his conception, if not the moment she had first laid eyes on that morose tinkerer, she insisted that if his life had been determined at all, it was by the story he chose to tell about it—a tale of fish tank design and depression that could not help but come to fruition—and not by the genes he had inherited from his father, who, she maintained to the day of her son's death, was an exuberant industrialist.

83

BETRAYAL

....

Earlier this year we attended a performance of our friend's one-man show, *Dr. Horowitz, D.D.S.*, which he, Max, had described to us as the "definitive takedown" of his father, the Dr. Horowitz of the title. Max had warned us that the show, which was being put on in the multipurpose room of an Armenian church, would not hold back "whatsoever." It would, he said, *destroy* his father, *devastate* his family, and *ravage* modern dentistry. Our friend's "total commitment to art" prevented him from sugarcoating the truth about his father, one of our suburb's most beloved pediatric dentists.

"It is seventy-five minutes of betrayal and brutalization, plus a ten-minute intermission," Max told us just before the first performance.

But the show we saw that night would be better described as an extraordinarily tender portrayal of a skillful dentist and loving family man.

His father, visibly moved, led us in a standing ovation. The multipurpose room of the Armenian church resounded with applause.

To this day Max remains bewildered by the response to his show. "I actually do not understand why my father's still speaking to me," he said. "After I annihilated him."

84

DISAGREEMENT

. . . .

Considering the divergent paths their lives had taken, a son whose father had bequeathed to him his extensive collection of books was not surprised to find that his father's library did not overlap whatsoever with his own. What he owned his father did not, and what his father owned he did not. He was not *surprised*, but upon shelving his father's books beside his own he was still moved to tears by the sight of these nonoverlapping libraries, a stark symbol of the gulf between them.

Some years later, though, while absentmindedly scanning his shelves, he noticed that he had two copies of the same slim black book, a book he only faintly remembered reading, the memoirs and maxims of a nineteenth-century German polymath. One copy had his own name scribbled on the inside cover and the other had his father's name scribbled in the very same place. Sensing that he had stumbled upon some secret subterranean channel connecting his father's mind to his own, which would render all of the apparent differences between them superficial and inconsequential, he snapped the spines of both books and lay them flat on his desk, open to the same page.

At first the annotations looked quite dissimilar. Then he realized, rifling rapidly through the pages, that they were absolutely, flawlessly dissimilar. What his father had underlined he had not, and what he'd underlined his father had not. Where his father in the margins had put a single exclamation point, he had put a single question mark, and vice versa, and where his father had put two exclamation points he'd put two questions marks, and vice versa. Where one wrote *Yes*, the other wrote *What*, where one wrote *No* the other wrote *Self-evidently true*, where the first wrote *Huh?*, the second wrote *Sounds like Socrates (in the Apology)*, and where the second wrote *Huh?*, the first wrote *Sounds like Socrates (in the Apology)*. Wherever the father had written *cf. Weber's Protestant Ethic*, the son had written *Tendentious*, and the father's *Tendentious* was likewise associated in every instance with the son's *cf. Weber's Protestant Ethic*. Wherever the son had put *Very clever little argument!*, his father had written *This sort of thinking led directly to the Holocaust* and, needless to say, the arguments that the father considered very clever were precisely those that the son believed led directly to the Holocaust.

He could, of course, have seen these disagreements in a negative light, as yet another symbol—even the definitive symbol—of the infinite void that yawned between them. But, as it happens, the son was powerfully moved by the comprehensiveness, the exactitude, the *perfection* of the disagreement here with his father. In fact, he had never felt closer to him.

SHIMURA'S ROBOT

....

The inventor Shimura's much-anticipated robotic father—which was designed to provide orphanages with a paternal presence, albeit a humanoid one—has turned out to be a total disaster. Mostly he ignores the orphans. Every fifteen minutes he raises one of his robotic arms and violently hushes the entire orphanage. He consumes the biographies of business titans, which, according to the manual, are actually scanned via the eyes and downloaded onto his massive hard drive. Shimura seems baffled by the negative response to his robot, which has led to speculation about his childhood.

HUMAN CONSUMPTION

....

Until Thursday, the Hirsch Company had produced its artificial food dye—used mainly to color sausage casings—continuously since 1868, when it was synthesized by the Breslau-born chemist Felix Hirsch. Hirsch got fantastically rich off the chemical. On his deathbed he summoned his eldest son, who was about to inherit both the fortune and the company, and confessed, in an agonized tone which his son had never heard before, that the synthetic dye was poisonous to human beings. In large quantities it shut down major organs, brought on huge tumors, caused the heart to rupture.

His son was struck dumb.

"Say something," his father begged.

The son murmured, "How long have you known?"

All along, Hirsch admitted. From that winter morning in 1868 when he had first synthesized the chemical. He was weak, he said. He was corrupt. He wanted money; he wanted his *family* to have money. Until this moment, he had not told a soul.

But his son was free to do with the knowledge as he pleased. "Expose me," whispered Felix Hirsch. "Repudiate me." His last words were: "Renounce me."

But the son decided to say nothing. His father remained a chemical hero, the Hirsch Company kept churning out gallon upon gallon of the poisonous orange dye, and the Hirsch family continued to live in luxury. In fact, the son cornered the global market for sausage casing coloration, driving out of business the organic, immensely salubrious dyes manufactured by his competitors. But on his deathbed, wracked with guilt, he summoned his son, the new chairman, and told him the family dye killed organs, caused tumors, and exploded hearts.

His son was aghast. "How long have you known?"

"All along."

"It *explodes hearts*?"

"Yes," said the father. "Tell the world."

But the son told no one. His grandfather remained a chemical hero, his father was considered a business legend, casings around the globe continued to be colored by Hirsch dyes, and the family fortune grew without bound. And as he died he mentioned to his son the organ-killing, tumor-causing, heart-exploding properties of the family dye and encouraged him to come clean.

A dynastic pattern had been established, and whenever such a pattern has been established—son *inherits* sausage casing colorant, son *learns truth* about lethal nature of casing colorant, son nevertheless *exploits to the fullest* the financial potential of colorant, son *divulges truth* about colorant to his own son and moments before death counsels him to confess the family's crimes to the public—it is actually very hard to break. So it happened that the Hirsch family continued making their noxious dye for nearly 150 years, causing tens of millions of organs to fail, tens of millions of hearts to explode, and tens of millions of tumors to grow to unbelievable sizes. If the dye consumer did not die of organ failure or heart explosion, his big, abundant tumors would impinge on the few organs that did survive and bring about the most gruesome death imaginable. Yet so many other chemicals caused similar problems in the period between 1868 and now that these deaths were never traced back to the sausage casings or from the sausage casings to the dye. Till last week, only the Hirsch fathers and sons knew the truth. They inherited their death toll reluctantly, they invested their death toll prudently, they watched their death toll grow by several percentage points a year, and in the end they left their death toll and all of its ethical considerations to their sons.

Last week, of course, saw the publication of the first study to suggest that Orange 6, the colorant in certain sausage casings, is toxic. Researchers fed a large quantity of these casings to twenty rats, all of whom died, twenty cats, all of whom died, and twenty dogs, all of whom died instantly. Then three hundred white mice died after ingesting the casings. In a final round of testing, eleven monkeys were fed an extract of Orange 6 mixed with milk. The monkeys died.

The public outcry was immediate and intense. Yet the current head of the Hirsch Company, Adam Hirsch, stood by his family's product. The dye, he insisted, is absolutely safe for human consumption. To prove it, he pledged to eat one thousand sausage casings on a platform in the center of the Hirsch Family Atrium, home, as it happens, to one of the finest bonsai collections in the Western hemisphere.

There has been plenty of speculation about his motives. Some say his father, who died young, failed to pass on the family secret. Others believe Hirsch had been told that the dye was toxic but couldn't believe it, couldn't believe that his family was capable of such villainy. A third camp thinks Hirsch had been told the secret, believed it, and wanted to atone for the family sins in a "poetic" manner, by eating a bunch of his own colorant and suffering the consequences in public. Whatever the reason, that is what happened Thursday in his family's atrium, surrounded by their stunted Japanese trees. After 70 sausage casings his spleen shut down, after 110 casings his kidneys failed, and as he ingested his 233rd casing, his heart exploded. When his body was cut open by the coroner it was found to be filled with tumors.

The company, headed now by Adam Hirsch's son, has issued a press release announcing that it would halt production of Orange 6 temporarily, pending further study of its possible effect on the human body.

STUNT

. . . .

A Las Vegas illusionist who rose to fame in the 1980s and '90s with a series of televised stunts—including jumping from an airplane without a parachute, hanging upside-down from a crane in Times Square for forty-four hours without a safety net, and crossing the Grand Canyon on a high wire without a harness—pitched last week to ABC, NBC, and CBS a stunt in which he would discuss politics and modern-day society with his octogenarian father for ten straight hours, without, he said, a safety harness. He would discuss power, money, unions, war, Social Security, human nature, anti-Semitism, and the JFK assassination, among other topics, with his elderly, extremely frustrated father for ten hours without a break, and with no harness. At the end of the discussion, he would jump onto a landing platform, where he would receive careful medical attention. The illusionist called it his "greatest stunt yet," though all three networks ultimately passed on his pitch.

THE PERFORMING ARTS

. . . .

Last year we read about the enormous bequest, rumored to exceed $50 million, that promised to rescue the Metropolitan Opera from the brink of insolvency. This year the bequest was challenged in court by the benefactor's son, a self-described actor, spoken-word poet, and performance artist, who claimed that his father had never shown any interest in opera, or, indeed, any of the performing arts. His lawsuit claimed that his father had been manipulated by his third wife, whom the son referred to only as "the Russian woman," into removing him from the will and funneling his former inheritance toward the opera—an art form the father, according to the son, had never understood or appreciated.

Opera supporters feared the worst. The son's case seemed solid, especially since the father was mentally enfeebled in his last year, when the will was changed.

But the court proceedings took a strange turn.

The son's lawyers, the most talented team of litigators in the country, focused at first on arcane aspects of estate law and appeared, as anticipated, to be winning the case. The Metropolitan Opera looked to be doomed. But after week one of the trial, the son fired all of his lawyers and insisted on arguing the case himself. He called himself to the stand and interrogated himself at length about the high school performance of *The Music Man*, twenty years prior, in which he had played Harold Hill. His father, who had promised to attend, went instead on a last-minute business trip to London and missed all four performances, including the Saturday matinee.

The son then called to the stand a musical theater expert and asked him a single question: Was, or was not, Harold Hill the main character in *The Music Man*?

He was, the expert said.

The judge ruled all of this testimony irrelevant and inadmissible and ordered the son to pursue a more pertinent line of questioning. When the son refused to speak about anything other than *The Music Man*, the size of the Harold Hill role, and the last-minute London business trip, the judge held him in contempt of court and threw out the lawsuit.

The dramatic way in which the son was dragged from the courtroom, screaming about a classmate who played a mere townsperson of River City but whose father had managed to attend all four performances, led some to suspect that his entire case had been a piece of performance art. In a coy interview this month the son seemed to imply as much, and hinted that he'd always intended for his "brothers and sisters in the opera" to keep his father's money. Others believe this to be an obvious face-saving tactic; opera supporters, in particular, have scoffed at the son's ex post facto attempt to turn the trial into some sort of modern art piece. At any rate, the Metropolitan Opera remains, to their relief, flush with funds, and has supposedly lined up a spectacular season, ending with Wagner's *Lohengrin*.

{ 89 }

IN SYMPATHY

....

The son of a famous Swiss strongman was born with a suite of physical deformities. His father, who'd once been able to clean and jerk 173 kilograms, felt now that his enormous, powerful body was an obscenity, and in sympathy for his son he let it waste away, in fact rather dramatically. Soon the sympathetic strongman was nearly as weak as his son, then he was just as weak as him, and shortly thereafter he dropped dead. The coroner actually wrote down as the cause of death: *Strongman's sympathy for son*. Needless to say, when the son grew up and found out what had happened to his father, he developed—in addition to the suite of physical deformities—a set of mental disorders.

{ 90 }

THE FOURTH SONATA

. . . .

A German composer whose earliest songs and sonatas had been dismissed as trifling and derivative, and whose father had begun to suggest, in his exceedingly gentle way, that he look into business or the law, went in 1924 to live in a timber hut beside a lake in the north of Finland, where over the course of several years, in perfect solitude, he pioneered an ingenious method of composition, very, very different from Schoenberg's chromaticism, if superficially of course somewhat similar to it.

He returned to Leipzig in 1927 with his Piano Sonata No. 4, imagining the whole way home his father's teary-eyed rapture when he plopped down at the family's little upright piano and played for him, quite casually, his groundbreaking new piece. But upon his arrival he discovered, to his horror, that in consequence of a locomotive whistle sounding too close to his head his father had gone, at some point during the son's Finnish sojourn, completely deaf.

Unable to play the piece for his father, the composer cast about desperately for other means of transmitting its essence into his father's head. First he described the piece, its theoretical innovations, the crucial ways in which it diverged from Schoenberg; next he asked his father to observe please the faces of two delighted listeners; then he had him place his cheek to the piano as he played the piece in order to feel its vibrations. Yet none of this was capable of actually transmitting the *essence* of the piece into his father's head, even though that head was constantly nodding and smiling and producing statements like: "I'm sure it's a very nice piece, and not just nice but important."

Finally the composer came to recognize that his sonata could only be absorbed as art, not as theoretical explanation, secondhand observation, or cranial vibration. And while art for the ear could no longer reach his father, there was still, was there not, art for the eye.

Yes, he would get his art into his father's head through the front of it rather than the two sides. Forget the sides, he thought, reinvigorated. The front! The front!

He returned to his Finnish hut in 1928, committed to inventing a visual idiom that would let him communicate to his father, in a painting, the essence of Piano Sonata No. 4. Not since grade school had he held a paintbrush. But after two years of arduous study he had mastered the basics, and after two more he had translated his musical idiom into a corresponding visual one. At this point he sent a letter to his mother asking simply, "How is Father's vision?" She sent an effusive loving letter in return, filled with maternal irrelevancies, but noting at the end that Father's vision was fine and he was excited to see the painting. In his fifth year in the hut the composer painted his colossal *Composition IV*, which expressed perfectly the essence of his fourth sonata. Carefully, very laboriously, he transported the canvas back to Leipzig, bent over beneath its weight for the final leg from the train station home. His mother opened the door grimly. Behind her his father hobbled toward them with a cane, one eye milky white, the other covered by an eyepatch.

"I'm so sorry," she whispered.

"I understand you have made a very nice painting!" his father shouted. "And very important!"

Back at the Finnish hut the composer contrived a third way into his father's head. The sides were blocked, as was the upper part of the front, but there was still, he realized, lower down on the same plane, his father's nose, and tongue. He learned to cook, transposing the inner essence of his fourth sonata into a meal for his father to ingest, but returned to Leipzig to find that the old man—though filled with encouraging words for his son's cookery—was fed now a prescribed paste by tube to the stomach and could not himself taste it.

His father's head was wholly closed off to him. Every ingress was occluded, ears to nostrils. His final stay in the Finnish hut was spent ruminating darkly on his father's impermeability to his art. One morning he filled his pockets with heavy stones and strode into the lake. But at the moment the water reached his neck, he suddenly stopped. Perhaps, he thought, the endless, fruitless attempt to transmit to his father the essence of his art *was* the essence of his art.

He emptied his pockets and hurried down to Leipzig, where with a fingertip he pressed, letter by letter, this epiphany into his father's palm. His father, robbed of almost every sense and recently of speech, responded by grabbing his hand and squeezing it tightly and rapidly, again and again, like the contractions of the heart, for minutes on end. The composer couldn't tell, of course (and this was now a part of his art), whether he had understood completely or completely lost his mind.

PARTIAL TEMPLES

....

The son of a certain king in the Davidic line was astonished and a little irritated when his father—already in his seventh decade—announced plans to build an immense temple out of white marble in the center of the city.

"You watch," the son told his attendant. "*I* will have to finish building that huge marble temple."

It was true. After only a quarter of the immense marble temple had been built, the king keeled over, dead. His son became the new king. But instead of completing the vast marble temple his father had begun, he decided to abandon it and begin building his own immense marble temple right beside it.

Construction went on smoothly for thirty years. Then, one day, with the immense marble temple about halfway done, the king dropped dead. The new king, his son, halted construction on the old temple and announced plans to erect a new temple—also of white marble, also immense, also in the city center—right beside his grandfather's abandoned quarter-temple and his father's abandoned half-temple. He oversaw the construction of two-fifths of a temple before he was poisoned by his son, now known, aside from regicide, for building a third of an immense marble temple in the center of the city. This son's son, in turn, declared himself "The Temple Builder." He built two-ninths of a new marble temple—very vast and very central—before he died. After his death, there was a struggle for power. Each of the king's three sons anointed himself his father's successor, and each built a fraction of an immense white marble temple (a sixth of a temple, a half a temple, and three-sevenths of a temple, respectively) before they slaughtered one another.

Now a very powerful king arose, the eldest son of the second son. "I shall build a temple," he told his people. "Not like those of my father and forefathers, responsible for these ruins that lie before you. No, my temple shall be *immense*. It shall be located in the *center of the city*. And it shall be made entirely of *white marble*." He built three-eighths of a temple.

His son abandoned his father's temple and built a fifth of his own marble temple. His son built four-ninths of his own immense white marble temple. His son abandoned the temple his father had begun and—importing white marble from the finest quarries in the known world—commenced construction of his own, right beside the others.

This king's son was a student of history. It is said that he sat for nineteen years in the Library of Alexandria, refusing to leave until he had read every book there. When he finally came home, he stood on the balcony of his father's palace and looked out over all these partial temples that littered his city. According to some texts, he wept. "When I am king," he told his attendant, "I will finish building my father's temple."

But, for reasons that were not recorded, when his father died, leaving five-sixths of a temple and instructions for how it ought to be completed, the son abandoned it and started building his own vast marble temple. He built two-sevenths of it and died young, mere weeks after the birth of his son (a quarter of a temple).

92

CAPITAL

....

In 1936, Walter Rosenthal of the eponymous banking empire began searching urgently for a way to smuggle his family's fortune out of Vienna. To carry it out as cash or gold, stocks or bonds, was impossible. At last, according to a family chronicle written by Rosenthal's great-grandson, he hit upon the notion of smuggling it out as human capital. Rosenthal liquidated his banks and purchased humanistic educations for his four sons at the Sorbonne. One son studied Spinoza, another Romanticism, another Romanesque architecture, and the last Greek tragedy. Within a few years, all of his economic capital had been converted into wisdom, subtlety, irony, and prestige, which were then stashed (in the form of humanities professors) at four different American college campuses. According to the family chronicle, Rosenthal prudently stored half his capital (converted to humanists) on the West Coast, and the other half (also as humanists) on the East Coast. By the time Hitler's tanks rolled into Paris, Rosenthal's fortune was securely distributed across the

United States, teaching art history survey courses and serving on departmental committees.

Naturally these humanities professors birthed other humanities professors, who in turn birthed humanities professors of their own, all of whom wrote books and essays and attended interesting events and formulated clever cultural critiques, thereby growing Rosenthal's wisdom, subtlety, irony, and prestige empire at approximately the same rate it would have grown over the same period had it remained a financial empire. According to the family chronicle, the latest generation of Rosenthal humanists, writing in the wake of the 2008 recession, has been severely critical of capitalism, not realizing that they themselves, while ostensibly Jewish studies professors, comparative literature professors, sociologists of the workplace, and historians of capitalism, constitute in reality the capital stock of the Rosenthal dynasty. The chronicler himself, of course, as he notes, is in a particular bind: he would like to be critical of his family, but his every thought, no matter how critical, only contributes to the Rosenthal hoard of wisdom, subtlety, irony, and prestige, which could—in the course of just one generation—be converted back into cash.

93

STRASSBERG & STRASSBERG

....

The Strassberg brothers, though easily among the most talented of the Brill Building songwriters, were never able to reproduce the success of their late 1950s hits "Good Girl (I Need You Bad)" and "Lookin' for a Woman," both recorded by Big Jim Harrison and the High Flyers, in part, according to a recent biography of the brothers, because Harrison and other Brill Building singers grew concerned about the lyrical direction their love songs seemed to be taking. In 1958's "Good Girl (I Need You Bad)" the Strassbergs wrote of a "Girl in Kansas City, standing five foot three / I feel a million miles tall, when she's standing next to me." By 1959, in "Lookin' for a Woman," they were writing about a "San Francisco baby, 'bout five foot five / toolin' round the city, she's gonna teach me how to drive." Despite the success of these songs, which reached number three and number eight on the charts, respectively, Harrison declined to record their 1960 song "Drown You in Kisses," featuring the lyric, "Love me a woman, almost six feet tall / big ol' beard, she tossin' me a ball / Yeah, gonna drown you in kisses, but don't you fear / I'm gonna toss you a life raft, you and your beard." That same year they approached an up-and-coming doo-wop group called the Sliders with a love song called "Bristly, Big, and Black," which began: "Long Island baby, Hungarian American Jew / Six feet tall, taciturn, big ol' beard too / Tuck me in, baby, the way you did way back / Her beard ticklin' my cheek, bristly, big, and black / Oh yeah / Her beard was bristly, big, and black."

The song failed to make the charts.

After the fiasco of "Bristly, Big, and Black," the Strassbergs went into seclusion, as the biography recounts. Their music publisher, Brill Building legend Al Kushner, tracked them down eventually to a dilapidated trailer in the woods of Maine. They lived knee-deep in sheet music: hundreds of love songs about this tall, resolute, very reserved, sixty-year-old Hungarian American "woman," almost metaphysically lonely, sporadically emotive but for the most part inscrutable, with her big scratchy black beard. Kushner told them: Boys, I know exactly where you're coming from. I come from there, too. These are my kind of love songs, but they're not the kind my singers wanna sing or America wants to hear. If you can write me one of *those*, though, if you can somehow harness this source of inspiration of yours and use it to produce a regular little love song, a song about romantic love, set to one of your snappy Strassberg melodies, I promise you I'll make it a number one hit.

The Strassberg brothers worked through the winter and

spring, and in June of '62 they marched into the Brill Building with the music and lyrics for "Come Home in Your Woman's Dress, Baby" ("Been leavin' the door unlocked for you, baby / Last night I dreamed you appeared / So beautiful, so short, such a woman / A woman's face, no beard / Tell me you love me, baby / Wearin' that dress I can't hardly bear / Tuck me in like you used to / Wearin' your dress like a woman would wear / Come home in your woman's dress, baby / I've been missin' you, missin' your nearness / Come home in your woman's dress, baby / Been missin' your face, completely beardless"). Lee Richards & the Robots took it to number thirty-nine on the Billboard Hot 100—a comeback of sorts, but not the comeback they'd hoped for.

Al Kushner summoned the Strassberg brothers to his office. I can do a whole helluva lot, he said, but one thing I cannot do is take a song about your father's beard and turn it into a top-ten hit.

The song is about romantic love, insisted the older Strassberg. The romantic love a man feels for a regular woman, no beard.

No beard, said the younger Strassberg.

I have to let you boys go, said Kushner. I wish you the best.

The biography loses sight of the Strassberg brothers not long afterward. They're heading out of Manhattan in a Volkswagen van, the younger driving, the older strumming a guitar in the passenger seat. Jim Harrison of the High Flyers saw them last. They waved to him at a stoplight up at Seventy-Ninth and Riverside, rolled down the window, sang him a couple of lines about an Austro-Hungarian immigrant with his Austro-Hungarian beard, his Jewish American convictions and his Jewish American fears, and then rolled up the window and turned onto the Henry Hudson Parkway, heading north. They were smiling, Harrison recalled some fifty years later. They seemed happy.

{ 94 }

DOUBTS

....

Three philosophers dying in three adjacent rooms at the Sloan Kettering Cancer Center each believed he had cracked, at the last minute, an ancient philosophical problem, and each instructed the nursing staff not to admit his respective son until he'd written down the solution. The first philosopher believed he had located at last the seat of the soul (it was attached to the underside of the neocortex). The philosopher in the second room believed he had solved the problem of ethics, with a kind of modified Kantianism. And the philosopher in the third room finally understood, after a lifetime of cogitation, how a part is related to the whole.

The three sons, waiting in the waiting room, made a pact: when each was let in to his father's room, he would raise no objections to his father's ridiculous deathbed theory, thereby allowing his father to die with serenity and a sense of his life having had purpose.

The first philosopher's son was admitted first. But he could not stop himself from immediately raising ten very vigorous objections to his father's neocortical theory of consciousness, and his father died in a state of extreme agitation.

Then the second son was let in to see his father, the moral philosopher. For more than three hours he showed nothing but enthusiasm for his father's ethical theory, but a minute before the old man died he suddenly posed a single devastating question, and his father died in a state of complete disillusionment.

The third son saw the first two emerge from their fathers' rooms in tears, having seen off their fathers in states of extreme agitation and complete disillusionment, respectively. He knew that he, too, would fail to suppress his skepticism when presented with his father's "solution" to a long-standing metaphysical conundrum. He was actually plotting his escape from the cancer center when the nurse opened the door to his father's room and said he could go in now. Inside he could see his father holding up his left hand, eager to show him how the fingers, for example, are related to the fist.

{ 95 }

REGRET

....

He had done everything possible to avoid going into his father's line of work. He studied something radically different. He moved far away from home. Yet now, years later, not a day goes by without him seeing a pregnant dog and thinking: I wish I could help you. (His father was a dog obstetrician.)

{ 96 }

POIGNANT

....

Late in life, Tom Browning, Ireland's most famous deaf and blind man, published a slim but hugely moving memoir called *My Father and Me*, about the man who had raised him when he was a small boy. The sensorium of his memories is unique: rather than the sight or sound of his father, rather than their conversations, Browning recalls "the touch of his palm, sometimes smooth and dry, sometimes damp, sometimes smeared with cream," or the "vast assortment of scents that indicated he was near—and he was always, it seemed to me in those days, near." So marvelous was this little book, miraculous in its very existence, that no one had the heart to tell Browning that he was raised not by his father (whom he never met) but by the thirty nuns of Saint Clare's Monastery, in Kilkenny. It was felt that this error did not diminish but actually contributed to, or was even exclusively responsible for, the book's poignancy.

97

MIDDLE GROUND

....

An eminent anthropologist at our university rose to fame in the 1960s with a monograph on the hitherto unknown South American tribe of Y., with whom he had lived for nearly seven years. He described the tribe as violent and irrational, inclined by nature to maim and murder at the slightest provocation.

Thirty years later, his son—who inevitably became an anthropologist himself—visited Y. (against his father's wishes) and produced a revisionist account, depicting the tribe as supremely peaceful and reasonable.

The son now rose to fame, while the father fell rapidly into disregard.

A long and painful estrangement ensued.

At last, at the son's urging, they returned to Y. together to resolve the dispute. The instant they stepped off their boat they were attacked by the people of Y., who hacked off the father's head and left the son paralyzed from the neck down.

The quadriplegic son, now kept alive by modern science,

recently announced that he would be writing another book, a book that would synthesize his father's findings and his own. His father had overstated the tribe's violence and irrationality, while he himself may have exaggerated their placidity and rationality. Now, by operating the computer on his wheelchair with his tongue, he plans to write an account that strikes a middle ground, halfway between their two positions.

98

THE BRENTANO TALES

. . . .

The Brentano Brothers, who aside from the Brothers Grimm were the most prolific of the nineteenth-century anthologizers of peasant folklore, have been accused in recent decades of not only sanitizing these tales, taming their brutality, but also of transforming every father, in the final paragraph of every tale, into a root vegetable—a potato, carrot, turnip, or beet—full still of moral certainties, from whom the son "had never felt more distant," and whom the mother eyes for a planned soup. These root vegetable transformations *were not present in the original tales*, according to folklore researchers who recently discovered in Palermo a trove of material that the brothers drew upon as a source, thus resolving some enduring mysteries of their work (why, for example, so many father characters are introduced in the second-to-last paragraph, only to be turned almost immediately into root vegetables, and then into soups, soups full still of moral certainties). These researchers have announced plans to publish a new edition of the Brentano Brothers tales with the violence and cruelty of the original material reinstated, and the father-to-root-vegetable transformations eliminated altogether.

99

THE BOSNIA PROJECT

· ·

An embittered screenwriter hammered into his son from a young age the simple, sad fact that Hollywood is run by businessmen, not artists. His whole career he'd been subject to the whims of the most ignorant, the most shortsighted, the most mercenary, and the most superficial men and women, products for the most part of Harvard Business School, who with their crude, knee-jerk judgments had refused again and again to produce the one script he had ever written that had any actual artistic merit, his project about the Bosnian War.

Don't follow my path, he told his son. If you want to make movies, make *money*.

The son did not need to be told twice. The indignities his father had suffered over the Bosnia script—a work of undeniable genius—had left a profound impression on him. The son studied finance, not literature, went to Harvard Business School, not film school, and took a job at a private equity firm. All along, he nurtured a secret fantasy: years from now, having taken over a movie studio, he would burst into a hospital room and whisper into his dying father's ear, "Dad, we're doing the Bosnia project."

Slowly but surely, as they say, that dream came true. He made a ton of money in New York and converted it effortlessly into Los Angeles power.

Fifteen years later he stood in his opulent office at Paramount, his father's Bosnia script in hand. Sadly, the script, which he had read probably ninety-nine times in childhood, awed every time by its genius, now, on the hundredth read, the first not to take place under his father's roof, was revealed to be complete garbage. Only when we have money and power of our own, thought the son as he drove to the hospital where his father lay dying, can we read our father's work honestly and see it for what it is, garbage not genius. That is the sad fact. Under his roof our father's work looks like genius, but under our roof, or our company's roof, it is revealed to be garbage. People like my father think money and power distort everything, he thought en route to the hospital, but really they make everything clear.

100

THE FLYING CONTRAPTION

....

A nineteenth-century Italian aristocrat who died trying to pilot his homemade flying contraption off a cliff in southern Tuscany, near Grosseto, instructed his wife with his final breaths to repair and to hang the contraption from a hook in their newborn son's nursery, in order to remind the boy of his father and his father's long struggle against the force of gravity, but not to allow him, under any circumstances, to actually fly the contraption.

She did as he wished. She hammered a hook into the ceiling of the boy's nursery and hung from it her beloved husband's flying contraption, which consisted of two bicycle pedals and a bicycle seat connected to a pinwheel of considerable size. And each morning when she plucked the boy from his crib, they had a little look at it. And she told him how clever his father had been, to attach the pedals and the seat to the pinwheel, and how brave, and how determined. What she respected most of all, she always told the boy, was that his father had been born rich and could have chosen a life of leisure, but instead he chose to struggle, and he chose to struggle against one of the greatest foes of all.

"Gravity," said the boy, when he was older.

"Yes, indeed, gravity," said his mother.

"But I must never fly it myself, right?" said the boy. "Because it isn't safe?"

"That's right," said his mother. "You must never fly the contraption yourself."

This made the boy sad. It made him sad, at first, because he wanted to be brave like his father! But later, when he had learned a little bit about aeronautics, it made him sad to think that his mother thought he would even be tempted to try to "fly" that thing. *Two bicycle pedals* attached to a *bicycle seat* attached to a *pinwheel*. Was his father, he often wondered as he stared at the contraption dangling on its hook, a stupid man, or an insane person, or both? Was his mother, who had never doubted his father's "struggle against the force of gravity," stupid, insane, or both? Had he inherited their stupidity? Their insanity? How much of his fortune had been squandered obtaining the pinwheel and connecting it to the pedals?

"You must never, ever try to fly the contraption yourself," his mother told him every single day, without fail.

"Got it, no flying the contraption," he replied. He wondered whether there was anything going on inside his mother's brain, or if she was more like an animal. "Contraption is a no."

As the years passed he came to resent the flying contraption more and more, this ridiculous and unsolicited intrusion of his father's—either stupid or insane—life into his own. He had nightmares of his stupid—or probably insane—father pedaling and falling, pedaling and falling, glancing up periodically with concern at the pinwheel. Meanwhile, his relationship with his mother suffered, grew false, based as it was on the foundational lie that his father's contraption was aeronautically compelling. He resented his father for building it, and he resented his mother for hanging it on a hook in his room. He resented his late father's absurd conviction in his flying contraption, and he resented his mother's equally absurd conviction in his father. He resented them, but he also felt sorry for them. He felt sorry for himself, too: for his modern condition. (By now he had read Nietzsche.) He would have loved to believe in anything as much as his stupid mother believed in his insane father, or as his insane father believed in his homemade flying contraption.

It is possible but not very interesting to trace the son's subsequent decline. In his journals, he attributes it to consciousness ("a psychological disease") and the contraption ("an aeronautical disease.") Consciousness, he writes, "works too well," while the flying contraption "does not work at all," but both of them "defy Nature." If only "the contraption worked as well as consciousness does, and consciousness worked as well as the contraption!" He was not really much of a philosopher, and in fact the father's flying contraption is now of more historical interest than the son's journals, which he privately dared to hope would lift him into the philosophical firmament. In any case, on an autumn night in 1898, he took the contraption off its hook (with the feeling, as he recorded in his final journal entry, that "this is what my father intended for me to do all along, to disobey my mother, to fly his contraption") and carried it to the very cliff where his father had died thirty years earlier. A butcher up at dawn to dismantle a pig happened to witness the son's flight. Apparently, before the contraption fell to earth, it generated a fair amount of lift. We cannot know if, for those few moments, as the pinwheel whirled and his father's contraption climbed through the air, the son reconsidered everything he thought he knew.

101

NORMALCY

....

One Czech modernist whose vast, loquacious, multifarious novels reached the end point of *profusion* in literature had a son who, upon realizing that his father had exhausted the possibilities of profusion, went to the other extreme, joining a Benedictine monastery in Orlová, near the Polish border, and exploring thereafter the possibilities of *silence*. Prior to taking his vow of chastity, however, he produced a son of his own, who upon his own self-described artistic awakening saw straight away that the only option remaining was a life of radically uncompromising *normalcy*, normalcy taken to the point of *absurdity*. He behaved normally, to the extreme, he spoke normally (to the point of absurdity), he lived in an apartment complex so rigorously normal in every dimension that it could legitimately be considered deranged, a deranged complex, on a street that was in some ways psychotically archetypal, he married a woman whom he called "the median woman of Prague," and in this meticulously normal context he wrote—in contradistinction to his loquacious modernist grandfather and his silent monkish father—

scrupulously normal books, with normal syntax, of normal length, on the most normal themes, thus pioneering and single-handedly exhausting a literature of normalcy, of the most stringent normalcy, a normalcy of great severity. His only departure, really, from a life of categorical normalcy was his refusal to give his wife the child for which she yearned, on the grounds that, after him, there would be no viable artistic strategies left for the little one; *his* was the last generation with a viable artistic strategy, as he explained.

TONE

. . . .

A man accused of sending rat-poison-coated razor blades to the biographers of his father, a recently deceased public figure, told the judge that he objected not to the content of the biographies but to their tone. The first biography, he said, was weirdly hostile, the second weirdly adulatory, and the third weirdly neutral. All three biographers received rat-poison-coated razor blades. When the judge asked whether he could imagine a biography of his father that would *not* warrant a rat-poison-coated razor blade, the man replied excitedly that he had actually had a dream the previous night that he had finished reading a new biography of his father and sent the author, instead of a razor blade coated on both sides with rat poison, a bouquet of flowers. But when he woke up he could not remember what the tone of this dream-biography had been.

PATRILINEAL

....

A brilliant geneticist who'd played a pivotal role in decoding the human genome was devastated when his only son, who had always, according to teachers, had "difficulty socializing" due to his "obsessive behavior" and his "periodic violent outbursts," was diagnosed with a rare psychiatric disorder. Pointing to the likelihood of future violent outbursts, his doctors strongly advised that the son be institutionalized, and the geneticist's wife, who lived in constant fear of these intermittent but always extremely violent outbursts, agreed with them.

The geneticist, however, flatly refused. It seems he had become fixated on the question of whether it was he or his wife who was genetically responsible for their son's troubled mind. Over the next decade, during which he and his wife were terrorized more and more frequently by their son's periodic outbursts, despite the antipsychotic drugs he was prescribed, the geneticist renounced all other scientific pursuits and even relinquished the directorship of his beloved institute in order to study his son's mind and genome, in comparison to his wife's and his own.

Again and again the wife begged him to have their son committed. But again and again the geneticist issued his refusal, typically by screaming the word *no*. He needed to determine, he said, whether it was he or she who was culpable for their son's troubled mind.

Finally, on a trip to Florence, standing in a long line to see Michelangelo's *David*, the son had an especially violent outburst and stabbed his mother in the heart with a ballpoint pen he had snatched from the hotel lobby. She died, and he was institutionalized at last.

For the geneticist, this was not only a horrifying *personal tragedy* but a profound *scientific setback*: in one fell swoop, he lost access to both his wife's mind and his son's mind. (He had, thankfully, complete copies of their genomes.) For a decade, he more or less disappeared. Neighbors reported loud sounds coming sporadically from his house. Twice the police came by to speak with him because he'd erupted, twice, at a neighbor's cat whom he accused—both times—of coming onto his lawn and looking at him through his windows. In civil moods, he explained to neighbors his "working hypothesis" that his son had inherited the mental disorder from the *maternal* side.

But just this year he reappeared at a conference at Cornell and triumphantly proclaimed that he'd isolated the gene that caused this rare psychiatric disorder. His son, he said, pointing at his own head somewhat insistently, had actually inherited it from the *paternal* side.

Two scientists I sat between at a dinner party last week told me that the geneticist will probably receive next year's Nobel Prize in Physiology or Medicine for his work on the patrilineal inheritance of the disorder.

DECISION-MAKING

....

The son of H. Philip Waldfogel—the chairman, under Ford, of the Federal Reserve, who had once had to decide between *expanding* the money supply, thereby reducing unemployment but raising inflation, and *contracting* the money supply, thereby reducing inflation but raising unemployment—can no longer bear to watch his father try to decide between the two desserts offered every evening at his Virginia nursing home. The choice is between cheesecake and mixed berry crumble. The son has requested that on evenings he visits, his father just be given the berry crumble, unless he explicitly asks for the cheesecake.

PHILANTHROPY

....

The heir to a huge food and beverage fortune, whose father, while he was alive, never gave one penny to charity, has announced that he will donate *all* of his father's assets to public health research on three terrible parasites. A third of his father's assets, said his press release, will go to research on "worms that enter the human body through the soles of the feet," a third will go to research on "worms that enter the human body through the whites of the eyes," and a third will go to research on "worms that enter the human body through the webbing of the fingers."

All of his father's assets, accumulated laboriously over the course of a lifetime, the press release concludes, will therefore be spent "all at once" on the study of worms entering the human body in three different places: the feet, the eyes, and the finger webbings.

While outwardly appreciative, the public health community was, needless to say, uniformly unnerved by the announcement. Many researchers, reluctant to involve themselves in a relationship they clearly did not understand, diplomatically declined the son's money. He, however, has insisted.

PRECISION

....

After forty years of arduous, isolated, often maddening scientific labor, a Slovenian physicist determined that the digit in the seventh decimal place of a certain fundamental physical constant, which his father had discovered and determined to six decimal places, and which was engraved to six decimal places on his father's gravestone, was a 9. He made a pilgrimage to his father's grave—located not in Ljubljana but in Vienna—and in a state of self-described "euphoria" attempted to chisel, with amateur instruments, under cover of darkness, a 9 at the end of his father's constant, in the seventh decimal place. But he managed only to crack the gravestone in two, and Vienna police arrested him on charges of vandalism. They simply could not understand that he wasn't trying to destroy his father's gravestone but to make it, as he said, "more precise." (As it happens, a team of South Korean physicists announced this week that the number in the seventh decimal place of the constant is not a 9 but a 4.)

AN ASYMMETRY

....

The lives of two sons had been dominated by the rivalry between their fathers, historians of the Holocaust, one of whom supported top-down explanations, and the other of whom advocated a bottom-up approach. Though one son, like his father, emphasized Hitler and Himmler, while the other son, like *his* father, stressed the complicity of the rank and file, they were similarly subsumed into their father's rivalry and had failed in almost identical ways to establish their own lives.

Finally, at forty, they conspired to send their fathers to the same retirement home, and specifically requested that the top-down historian be given a room just *beneath* the bottom-up historian.

The subtle irony of this retribution was sadly short-lived. Three weeks after the Holocaust historians had moved in, the home—later found to have violated countless building codes—suddenly collapsed, and the top-down historian's head was crushed by the bottom-up historian's bathtub. The bottom-up historian survived and is still with us. This has introduced an interesting asymmetry into the once symmetric situations of the two sons; it will be instructive to see if one or the other of them is able to salvage the second half of his life.

{ 108 }

GROOMED

....

The oldest son of a rich family—Jewish, incidentally—was being groomed to take over the family business, an industrial conglomerate. He learned from his father the vernacular, the social customs, and the substance, such as it is, of the business, and soon enough he could calculate the net present value of this or that investment, drink credibly with Korean shareholders, and speak with fluency and conviction the corporate patois of his forebears.

But the son did not have the physical presence of his father, did not have his monumentality, his height, his shoulders, his belly, all of which seemed indispensable to the position of chairman. And without these qualities (he began to fear) all the grooming in the world would come to nothing, he would let down his rich culturally Jewish family, and the diversified industrial conglomerate would collapse.

One afternoon, however, on the eve of the annual shareholders' meeting, his father summoned him to his office, instructed him to close the door, and, tugging upon a zipper elegantly concealed behind his right ear, actually began unzipping his entire body, revealing inside of it a small sentimental faultfinding octogenarian.

"Here, put this on," said the old man, handing the son the father's big, charismatic, broad-shouldered body. "No, no, not like that, not like that. Like *this*." He showed him how to step *firmly* into the father's foot and, working upward from ankle to knee, negotiating ligament and bone, how to secure the father's calf muscles around his own. Then he showed him how to wrap himself in the father's skin, proceeding bit by bit, keeping it uniform and taut, like tucking in a sheet.

"Are you sure," the son asked, referring to the body he'd now assumed up to the knees, "that you don't need this anymore?"

And the old man said, "I'll be fine, I'll be fine. Why don't you worry more about installing yourself in the pelvic girdle."

Indeed, that step *was* a little tricky, requiring some complicated contortions. The father did not make things any easier by intermittently yelping, "Be careful of the penis!" while spastically shooting out a withered arm to rescue that organ from whatever peril it seemed to him to be in. But once the son had mounted himself in his father's pelvis the process went a lot faster. He reached deep into his father's arms and shrugged on his father's torso, no differently than he would a winter coat. Then it was really just a matter of tightly swaddling his neck in his father's neck, donning his father's head like a helmet, stretching his father's face over the jawbone and around the back of the skull, and zipping it all up to the ear.

"Whoa," said the old man. "Who's this handsome guy?"

"Ha, ha," said the son.

"Who's this handsome guy, and what did he do with my son?"

"Very funny. I look okay?"

"Pretty spiffy. Let me look at you." The old man smoothed out a bulge in the son's spinal column and then reached a fist down the son's throat and flicked his uvula a couple of times with his middle finger. "Pretty damn spiffy, is what I think."

"It's a really nice body," the son said. "Thank you."

The sentimental octogenarian waved away the thanks, though the son thought he spotted tears welling in his eyes.

"Keep it clean," the old man said gruffly.

"I will."

"Be careful of the penis. Doorknobs, drawers, knives, car doors. Rotors."

"Of course."

The next morning the son, wearing his father's body, was introduced as the new chairman. The company's shareholders seemed to be reassured by his familiar presence, and the markets hardly registered the change. The stock price, which had been expected to fall slightly, in fact rose slightly, and the long-term outlook for the diversified industrial conglomerate remains the same as before.

UNFINISHED THINGS

....

On the brink of death an old man summoned his son and asked him to take care, after he was gone, of a few unfinished things.

Of course, said the son, trying not to sob. Anything!

With a tremulous finger the father pointed to a row of books on a shelf across the room, the six volumes of Edward Gibbon's *History of the Decline and Fall of the Roman Empire*. He'd read five of them, he said, but he had not had time to read the sixth. Life is astoundingly short! You can't imagine the regret you feel at the end of it. Please, he said, clutching his son's hand, finish it for me.

Of course! cried his son. I will, I promise!

Then the father handed his son a sheet of paper on which the words "The atom consists of" were typed at the top. He had always wanted to write a physical treatise, he said, and had even begun writing it—he pointed to the words "The atom consists of"—but life had interfered, and he had never completed it. Write the physical treatise, he said.

Oh, he added, and a biography of Gibbon, the man.

What? said the son.

My plan was to read *Decline and Fall* and then write a little biography of Gibbon, the man. Who *was* this guy, this parliamentarian-turned-historian, this classic "man of the Enlightenment"?

Um, said the son. Okay.

La, sang the old man. La. That was the first note of a symphony he had sometimes thought about composing, but had never composed. Please, he said, compose it.

He started coughing, and soon was gasping for air with a frantic look on his face. Oh my God, the son thought, this is it. But the old man managed at last to gather his breath, clear his throat, and request that his son track down and solve the biggest Rubik's Cube in the entire world, the biggest crossword puzzle in the entire world, and the biggest jigsaw puzzle in the entire world—ambitions the father, a puzzle dabbler of late, must have formulated pretty recently. Find them, he whispered with urgency, and solve them.

He had another coughing fit, and the son had the wrenching thought that it might perhaps be better for his illness to claim him now rather than prolong his suffering. But the fit subsided and the old man cried, So! and began ticking off the tasks on his fingers: read *Decline and Fall*, write the Gibbon biography, complete the physical treatise, compose the symphony, and solve the three extraordinary puzzles.

With that, the father closed his eyes. His breathing turned shallow, and after a few minutes it stopped altogether. The son was about to call for the doctor when his father abruptly opened his eyes, stared at him, and said in a loud, clear voice: Reforest the Earth.

{ 110 }

SANCTUARY

....

An embattled public figure, ridiculed on every side, returned home, expecting to find comfort at least *there*, but instead he found his son at the kitchen table producing one unflattering papier-mâché figurine of him after another. His hands still buried deep in gunk, the son insisted that the papier-mâché figurines depicted "men in general."

111

GROUNDWORK

·······················

The philosopher had spent forty years "clearing the ground" for a proper philosophy of mind. His philosophy, he said, was of an exclusively preparatory nature. It would be up to his students to construct the edifice on the ground he'd prepared, an edifice he would almost certainly not live to see.

He had also spent forty years clearing a plot of land he'd purchased in northern Vermont. He cleared brambles and cut down trees. But his landscaping was also of an exclusively preparatory nature: it would be up to his sons to erect the summer home on the ground he had prepared. He knew he would not live to see the summer home.

Though the philosopher claimed to be a fervent atheist, there was, undeniably, a great deal of faith at work here—or so we, his colleagues, whispered amongst ourselves. To live one's life in such an exclusively preparatory fashion, to always be clearing the ground, implied faith in one's followers, faith in life—even if not one's own—continuing after death, in a purpose greater than oneself, in a promised land worth sacrificing oneself for so that others might reach it. All of this groundwork, in philosophy as well as in northern Vermont (near Montpelier), essentially implied, we thought, a belief in God.

 When the philosopher fell ill he summoned his lawyer and made one last change to his will. Then he gathered his sons and students around his hospital bed, wished them well in their respective tasks, and died.

The lawyer read the will aloud: it left the philosophical ground that he had cleared to his sons, "upon which they shall construct a positive philosophical theory," and left the Vermont ground that he had cleared to his students, "upon which they shall construct a summer home."

There must be some mistake! cried the sons and the students. You mean that the philosophical ground goes to the students and the Vermont ground goes to the sons.

But there had been no mistake. The will plainly stated that the sons got the cleared philosophical ground and the students got the cleared Vermont ground, "and not the other way around."

A probate court judge upheld the validity of the will.

So the sons, who had no interest in philosophy and were not intelligent, started building a philosophical edifice, and the students, who had no interest in a summer home and were not handy, started building a summer home. Both the philosophical edifice and the Vermont summer home were grotesque, ramshackle structures that collapsed as soon as they were completed, injuring their architects and rendering totally unusable the ground on which they stood. It will probably be hundreds of years before anyone tries to clear the wreckage and construct another theory or another summer home on those particular spots.

We who knew the philosopher have puzzled over his bequest. One faction chalks it up to confusion, a second to mischief, a third to perversity, a fourth to malice, a fifth to ego. A sympathetic sixth group composed mostly of his students believes he lost his faith in his final days and realized his world would end with him. They sense regret, futility, a warning, a last lesson. A seventh group, his sons, thinks he'd simply had an undiagnosed stroke, after which he mistook his sons for his students and his students for his sons.

112

PARROT CARE

....

A statistician who, to keep him company after the untimely demise of his social worker wife, had purchased a young yellow-naped Amazon—a species of parrot well known for its high intelligence, its remarkable ability to mimic human speech, and its extremely long life span—stipulated in his will that his "wonderful bird" would go to his "wonderful son," as that son later related to us on the parrot care forum.

The son was, in fact, overjoyed to inherit the parrot, an affectionate creature who strutted happily about on his shoulders while uttering, in the precise pitch and tone of his father's voice, nearly two hundred phrases, including "Bayesian updating," "Null hypothesis," "Post hoc ergo propter hoc," and "I love you, sweetie bird." For reasons that the son has never really been able to articulate, he and his father had fallen increasingly out of touch in the years before his father's death, despite their absolutely unquestioned love for each other. Something about their relationship—here's the closest the son came to articulating it, and he felt that it articulated nothing at all—worked better in principle than in practice, he wrote us on the parrot care forum. In any case, he was devastated by his father's death and grateful to inherit the part of him preserved in the adolescent yellow-naped Amazon, who, when the son entered his father's dark apartment after the funeral, fluttered joyfully about his cage, repeating "Bayesian updating, Bayesian updating, Bayesian updating, So we can reject the null hypothesis" in the father's loud lecturing voice. "The normal aka the Gaussian distribution, I love you, sweetie bird!" cried the parrot, in the father's voice. The son burst into tears as he remembered his dad trying to interest him in these concepts many years ago, he told us later on the parrot care forum, and he contemplated the happy prospect of living the next fifty to sixty years with this companionable and actually somewhat sentimental tropical bird.

But the very moment the son maneuvered the cumbersome bird cage through his father's front door, toward the car, in order to begin the long drive back home, the formerly cheerful bird started to scream, also in the father's voice. The bird screamed the entire way home, always in the exact pitch and the exact tone of his father's voice. When they arrived home, the son set up the bird cage in the living room, hoping that that would be the end of it, but the bird stopped screaming only long enough to declare "The normal aka the Gaussian distribution!" before he started screaming again, in the father's voice. To this day, despite everything the son has tried, not only covering the cage with a sheet but even moving into his father's old apartment and resuming the study of statistics—although, as he informed us on the parrot care forum, he didn't know why he thought this might help—the parrot screams in the father's voice constantly, pausing only periodically to utter one of his two hundred statistical phrases. "Does anyone," the son asks the forum, now multiple times a day, even though he's exhausted our collective expertise, "have any tips for dealing with an adolescent yellow-naped Amazon that will not stop screaming (in my father's voice)?"

113

EXHAUSTION

....

A New York Abstract Expressionist who had moved alone in 1951 to the hills of North Carolina intended to produce a painting that would express everything he had to say about his father, and thus exhaust a theme that had sustained his early career but which, certain reviewers had begun carping, and he agreed with them, was artistically limiting, art-historically overworked, and fundamentally juvenile. One final painting, expressing everything there was to express about his father, and then he could finally move on, probably to political, racial, religious, sexual, or existential themes, if not straight to the Holocaust.

He stretched his canvas, dipped his brush, and began painting.

He anticipated, at first, an exceptionally *simple* painting: only a simple painting could possess the generality needed to encompass his father completely, to sum him up and thereby exhaust him. Just a few brushstrokes, he thought, and I'll be done.

But the resulting painting was *too* simple. It left out too much. It represented only one aspect of his father, one perspective on his father. He would need more brushstrokes, he realized, potentially a huge or even a shocking number of brushstrokes. I'll probably need, he said to himself, a disturbing or distressing number of brushstrokes, if I intend to exhaust my father as a theme and move on to politics, race, religion, sex, or existence, if not the Holocaust.

These new brushstrokes he began putting down in a frenzy, expressing, with a feeling of indescribable relief, more and more aspects of his father, from more and more perspectives, incrementally capturing his quintessence and exhausting him as a theme of any interest to the son. He layered stroke on stroke, color on color, and the painting took on a homogenous brown hue. He felt, as the painting became browner and browner, that his father was becoming gradually less interesting to him, and this he saw as a good sign. But he had to be careful! *Less interesting* was good but the painting wasn't finished until his father was of *absolutely no interest* to him at all—until his father was exhausted.

So, a couple months later, when a collector stopped by his studio up there in the Blue Ridge Mountains and offered him an enormous sum for the little canvas called *My Father*—by then a brownish, blackish square which, the very insecure collector proudly observed, was obviously indebted to Malevich—the artist turned him down, on the grounds that the painting wasn't finished yet.

He applied more brushstrokes, each one exhausting his father as a theme marginally more, until the painting was pitch-black. But his father, as a theme, was still not exhausted! So he continued to put down brushstrokes, capturing hitherto hidden aspects of his father from hitherto unconsidered angles, until the painting, through a complicated impasto technique of his own devising, began to protrude from the canvas and advance, as it were, toward the opposite wall of the studio, about thirty feet away, a black beam that exhausted his interest in his father little by little as it inched across the room at approximately eye level. The undeniably phallic nature of this new development proved irresistible to the painter's former friends, among them some of New York's most mediocre wits, who couldn't help but say things like, "I hear Podolsky"—for this was the painter's name—"I hear Podolsky is down there in the hills of North Carolina building a big black penis with which to express his father's essence," or, when they learned to their intense delight that the beam had grown precarious enough to require the support of three straps slung from the ceiling, "By strapping that big black penis to the ceiling Podolsky enables himself to continue articulating his father's essence."

He knew he was being mocked. And he mocked himself. From a 1962 letter to a sympathetic colleague in New Mexico: "You paint the same black beam, day in and day out, and after a year it's only grown a foot, and the total length of the black beam is nine feet after more than a decade of work—less than a foot of beam per year of work!—and the whole point of it is to exhaust your father as a source of perplexity and fascination, deplete him and turn him into any old object, so you can turn your attention elsewhere, but as of now he seems as inscrutable and metaphysically significant as ever—at what point do you start to wonder if you're losing your mind?" The colleague's sensible reply: "You're not losing your mind. You're making art. *Keep painting that beam.*" And, indeed, Podolsky's next letter finds him in a far more optimistic mood: "Just back from holiday with the folks. Like never before Father struck me as yr typical septuagenarian, now in bathrobe, now on couch, now walking in park, now sentimental, now frustrated, now eating his toasted sesame bagel as he reads his two-day-old newspaper. What once seemed permanently inexplicable now does not even need explaining. Either I have got near the bottom of this bottomless abyss, or the bottomless abyss was at the surface the entire time. Either way, I think the black beam is working. Thanks for yr encouragement."

That year the beam grew an unprecedented two and a half feet, and the artist had never been less interested in his father, though he could not yet honestly say that he was not interested in him at all. But by 1966 the black beam was seventeen feet long, more than half the length of the painter's studio, and Podolsky finally felt that he'd exhausted his father, that his father held no fascination for him whatsoever. He was, Podolsky felt, just a man, a very opinionated, frequently taciturn, sometimes maudlin man who happened long ago to be a consequential diplomat, but who was of no more artistic interest than anyone else. Smiling to himself, he thought: I've exhausted my father as a theme.

Only now did it occur to him how tragic that was, how *catastrophic.* After a brief moment of euphoria, of liberation, in which he began mentally sketching his next project (mixed-media Holocaust collage), he suddenly said aloud: "In a very real sense I have buried my father alive." Whether out of duty, guilt, or the realization that he actually had now a totally new perspective on his father, he picked up his brush and continued adding brushstrokes to that long black beam. In 1979, he punched a hole in the side of his studio and the beam, then thirty feet long, began jutting out into the Carolina hills. By the time the artist died of lymphoma in 2002, the black beam, which he'd retitled *Exhaustion,* was fifty-one feet long. Last year it landed in the permanent collection of the Tel Aviv Museum of Art, where, fondly referred to by a number of lewd nicknames, it has rapidly become a crowd favorite.

114

LAST WISHES

....

Nearing death, the famous Norwegian playwright came up with a brilliant if somewhat diabolical idea for his final work. He gathered his papers almost at random into two piles, one labeled "to burn" and one "to publish." Upon his death, his three sons, whom he had named as his executors, would come upon these papers and begin to argue over their proper disposition.

His oldest son, the playwright knew, would demand that they obey their father's last wishes to the letter, that is, to burn the "to burn" pile and to publish the "to publish" pile.

His middle son, who'd always believed that he understood his father better than his father understood himself, would want to burn the publish pile and publish the burn pile.

His youngest son, idolatrous of both his father and Literature, would insist upon publishing both piles.

A last request, a bitter family quarrel, the scent of burnt art: the public would be captivated, more so than the audience at any of his staged dramas. Real emotions would be generated, and his customary themes—fathers and sons, the incompatible obligations of family and art—would be articulated. After seven years, a press release would reveal that this feud over the last play was *itself* the last play, a tragedy for three actors entitled *Last Wishes*. He chose an epigraph from Ecclesiastes: "I hated all the things I had toiled for under the sun, because I must leave them to the one who comes after me. And who knows whether he will be a wise man or a fool?"

Having prepared everything, the playwright swallowed a cyanide pill and died. When his sons entered his study and found two piles, one labeled "to burn" and one labeled "to publish," they instantly, wordlessly, and harmoniously burned both piles, prodding and poking and jabbing at the ashes with their father's fire iron until there was nothing left. Then they went off to pursue quiet, private lives.

The playwright faded from public memory, and seven years later when a press release declared that "all of this over the past seven years" had constituted his last and greatest work, no one understood what "all of this" referred to, and the claim was met with confusion, derision, and pity.

LAST WORDS

....

My friend Theo's father, a professor of urban planning, suffered a massive stroke, after which he could utter only the two words *Theo* and *infrastructure*. For the last month of his life, these were the only words out of the father's mouth. Theo, who had always felt that he was a terrible disappointment to his father, was deeply moved that his name was on his dying father's lips. He took it as a sign that his father had finally forgiven and accepted him.

Years later, whenever we discuss these events, we simply pass over the fact that his father was saying not only *Theo*, but also *infrastructure*.

A MEMORIAL ON
THE RIVER HAVEL

. . . .

On the River Havel, near Wannsee, a talented young lawyer who was also a promising Expressionist poet fell through the ice and drowned. His inconsolable father and his very anguished friends both agreed that a statue ought to be erected on the banks of the Havel in his memory, but they could not agree on its design. Should the statue represent him in his capacity as a lawyer, as his father wished, or in his capacity as an Expressionist poet, as his friends wanted? In the end, they compromised. They commissioned and erected a statue of the young man—Heym—holding forth over the Havel; whether he was reciting a poem or presenting a legal argument was left to the spectator.

When, however, the friends convened at that tragic bend in the Havel on the second anniversary of Heym's death, they found that his father had installed, fifteen feet in front of the statue, in the middle of the river, a second statue, of a judge on his bench. This effectively closed off the possibility that the Heym statue was reciting a poem, and left no doubt that he was presenting a legal argument.

The friends, all of them Expressionist poets, were outraged. They rowed into the river and tried to topple the judge statue, then to vandalize it, but the thing was made of granite and virtually indestructible. Finally, they decided to pool their meager funds and commission three new statues: two figures seated six feet from the Heym statue, clearly poetry fans, listening raptly, and immediately behind them, back-to-back with them, an elderly lawyer addressing the statue of the judge. Now it appeared the Heym statue was reciting a poem to a small but avid audience, while nearby, in the shallows of the Havel, some lawyer was addressing a judge about an unrelated legal matter.

These granite statues were similarly unmovable and unbreakable. All the father could do now was install a statue of a poet between the first statue and the two seated poetry fans, so the poetry fans seemed to be listening to *that* poet, not to his son, as well as a statue of a stout woman and a dog between the new lawyer statue and the judge, so the lawyer seemed to be addressing not the judge but his stout wife and his loyal dog. On the pedestal of the judge's statue he had an engraver chisel, "Order in the courtroom! Counselor Heym, please proceed"— thus implying that the son's oral argument had been interrupted by the impromptu poetry reading and the sudden meeting-up of the elderly lawyer with his wife and dog.

After much deliberation, the friends commissioned a statue of a courtroom functionary looking at the judge while pointing at Heym with one hand and the elderly lawyer with the other hand, with an engraving on his pedestal reading, "Which Heym? They're both named Heym." But almost instantly Heym's father installed a statue of a second functionary pointing at the elderly lawyer, with an engraving reading, "No, his name is *Wurmbacher*." With that, the now-penniless Expressionist poets had to accept defeat. Heym's father's wealth was inexhaustible, they realized. And he was willing to spend all of it to determine his son's legacy.

Everyone involved in this story died and was more or less forgotten. But in the 1970s a circle of conceptual artists in Berlin—of which David Bowie was for a time on the periphery— rediscovered this emotional, illogical assemblage of granite statuary. It became a site of pilgrimage. When, in 1992, the German government announced that it would be razed to make way for a bridge over the Havel that would ultimately connect Berlin and Hannover by high-speed rail, a number of artists protested. These ten senseless and unsightly statues were part of the legacy of German modernism, they said. But the statues were torn down nevertheless, and today one can reach Hannover from Berlin in an hour and a half, a fact for which even the artists are grateful.

UNREST

....

One winter evening in 1905, on a street corner in Moscow, a radical who was carrying a bomb toward his tsarist father's home happened to bump into an acquaintance, a painter who was carrying a Symbolist painting toward his realist father's studio. On the far corner they spotted, purely by chance, a philosopher friend who was carrying an idealist manifesto toward his materialist father's office. The radical planned to kill his father, the Symbolist to surpass his father, and the idealist to refute his father. But when the radical, kneeling in his father's bathroom, armed his bomb, it went off prematurely and he killed himself instead. What happened to the other two is unknown.